Summer Promises

THE
SILVER BEACH
TRILOGY

Summer Promises

DIANE SCHWEMM

BANTAM BOOKS
NEW YORK • TORONTO • LONDON • SYDNEY • AUCKLAND

RL 6.0, AGES 012 AND UP

SUMMER PROMISES

A Bantam Book/June 2005
First Bantam Books Edition September 1995

ISBN: 0-553-56722-5

Visit us on the Web! www.randomhouse.com/teens
Educators and librarians, for a variety of teaching tools,
visit us at www.randomhouse.com/teachers

Published simultaneously in the United States and Canada

Bantam Books is an imprint of Random House Children's Books, a division of
Random House, Inc. BANTAM BOOKS and the rooster colophon are
registered trademarks of Random House, Inc.

Printed in the United States of America

OPM 10 9 8 7 6 5 4 3 2

For Eliot and Joshua

1

"I really can't wait to see you," eighteen-year-old Elli Wells told her boyfriend, Sam DeWitt, over the telephone on Saturday. "Are you sure you can't make it up to Silver Beach until the middle of the week?"

"Believe me, I'll get there as soon as I can," Sam promised. "And Elli, I . . ." His voice became low and husky. He'd never actually told her he loved her; Elli waited breathlessly. "I'm crazy about you," he said at last. "I can't wait for us to be together."

"Me either. Bye, Sam."

Elli hung up the phone, not really disappointed that Sam hadn't said it. *"I love you"—those are serious words,* Elli thought as she walked to the picture window in the living room of her father's Lincoln Park high-rise apartment. She looked down at the sea of green treetops, the sinuous curve of Lake Shore Drive, and Lake Michigan, its blue surface ruffled by the morning breeze. She wasn't necessarily ready to say it herself, and there was no rush. *We'll have all summer to explore our feelings for each other,* Elli thought, a delicious tingle chasing up her spine.

Hearing footsteps on the wood floor behind her, she turned. Arthur Wells stood in the entrance to the living room, briefcase in hand, checking his watch. "You're going into the office on a Saturday?" Elli asked.

"Just for a few hours, hon," her father replied. "But I suppose you kids will be gone by the time I get home."

"We'll probably leave before lunch," she confirmed. "It's a long drive."

"Well . . ." His face twisted in a wry smile. "Have a great summer. I'll miss you."

Elli crossed the room to give him a hug. "We'll miss you, too, Dad."

"Give my regards to your mother," he added somewhat formally.

"Sure, Dad. So long."

The door clicked shut behind him. Elli returned to the window and curled up on the sofa, resting her chin in her hand. After a few minutes her father appeared on the sidewalk far below. She lifted her hand in a wave, but he didn't look up.

"He's such a workaholic," a voice behind her remarked.

Elli turned. Her younger brother, Ethan, entered the room, dressed in boxers and a ripped T-shirt and holding a coffee mug.

"Yep. Always has been," she agreed.

Seventeen-year-old Ethan dropped into an easy chair and planted his feet on the coffee table. "Well, he hasn't always been *this* bad. He's gotten a lot worse since the divorce. He'll probably stay at the office all day. *And* go in tomorrow, too."

Elli sighed. "You're probably right. When was the last time he took a vacation?"

"Two summers ago at Silver Beach, I bet," Ethan said dryly.

Two summers ago, their parents had still been married, but things were starting to fall apart. "Some vacation that was," Elli recalled. "It wrecked their marriage for good."

Ethan sipped his coffee. "Would have happened sooner or later, don't you think?"

Elli shrugged. She still wasn't sure. Her parents had been divorced for almost a year, separated for a year before that; it seemed like centuries since they'd been a picture-perfect family of four. But had it really been inevitable? *At one point they were happy,* Elli thought. *At one point it worked.*

"I mean, the thing between Mom and Mr. Ransom," Ethan continued. "That was going on for years."

"Yeah, it was," Elli conceded. The previous summer, their mother had started dating their neighbor at Silver Beach, widowed novelist Holling Ransom. Halfway through vacation, Elli had made a shocking discovery: her mother's affair with Mr. Ransom dated back a decade. They'd been romantically involved at the time Annette Ransom drowned, and according to Charlotte Ransom, her mother hadn't drowned by accident—she'd committed suicide. Mrs. Wells was at the summer colony now, having driven up by herself the week before. "Maybe it *was* destined to happen this way," Elli added. "That's what Nana would say, anyhow."

"So." Ethan put a hand on the arm of the chair and pushed himself up. "Guess we should get ready to hit the road."

"Yeah." A tiny frown creased Elli's forehead. "But Ethan, are you . . . are you sure you want to go to Silver Beach this summer? I mean, Mr. Williams offered you that great job at the youth center. It's probably not too late to say yes. Wouldn't it be more fun to—"

"I'm going to Silver Beach," Ethan cut in, his voice sharp. As he turned to leave the room she thought she heard him mutter under his breath, "I couldn't stay away, even if I wanted to."

Alone again, Elli stared out the window, but this time she wasn't seeing the Chicago lakeshore. Images of Silver Beach swam before her eyes. What she'd told Sam on the phone was

4

true—she couldn't wait to get to Silver Beach, to see him, to spend the whole vacation together. Their romance had been rocky the previous summer, but they'd ended on a positive note, and over the winter she'd visited him a few times at college. The relationship had solidified; it was on the verge of becoming something serious, and there was nothing Elli wanted more.

But there was a flip side to the coin. Part of Elli wished that none of them, especially Ethan, would ever set foot in Silver Beach, Michigan, again. And the reason for that was named Charlotte Ransom.

Despite her mixed feelings, Elli couldn't help getting excited as the dark-green Range Rover drew near the small north Michigan resort colony of Silver Beach. "Nothing ever changes," she observed to her brother, who was slumped in the passenger seat, his bare feet on the dashboard. Her eyes drank in the rolling, green countryside. "Should we stop at the Jantzens' farm stand for some vegetables?"

"Nana knows we're coming—I'm sure she stocked up."

"Look," said Elli as they slowed down to pass through the village of Silver Glen. "The Gas 'n' Grocery has a new sign."

"Spiffy," said Ethan. "The rest of the shops in this hick town should take the hint."

Elli didn't agree. She liked the Glen just the way it was—Bailey's Bait and Tackle, Christabel's House of Beauty, Bee's Bakery, Harlan's Boat Repair, all stubbornly old-fashioned. "I wouldn't change any of it," she argued. "It's *real*. What you see is what you get."

Within moments they were in the country again. A few more miles, and the orchards and meadows gave way to a vista of sparkling blue: Lake Michigan. "What a day," Elli exclaimed. "Let's go for a sail right away, okay?"

The Range Rover bumped along the private gravel road leading into the exclusive, century-old summer colony. They passed the nine-hole golf course, tennis courts, yacht club and dock, and then the houses themselves: gracious, rambling Victorians with gingerbread turrets and wraparound porches presiding over perfectly manicured green lawns and gardens riotous with early-summer color. Their flags snapping in the breeze, the cottages faced the lake as they had for more than a hundred years, as they would for a hundred years more. A strange peace stole into Elli's heart. *Whatever crazy things go on in our lives, the changes, the heartbreaks,* she thought, *this place will always be there to hold us up. Battered by storms, maybe, like it was this past winter, but not growing older in the way that people do. Never dying.*

She steered the Range Rover into the driveway of an elegant gray-shingled cottage, parking next to her mother's Volvo and her grandmother's Lincoln Continental. "Hey, everybody," Ethan yelled, jumping out and reaching into the back for one of his duffel bags.

"We're here," Elli called.

They were answered by silence. Laden with suitcases, they stumbled up the porch steps. "Door's wide open—they can't be far," said Elli.

"The beach, probably," guessed Ethan.

As her brother hauled his bags upstairs Elli wandered around the first floor. Curtains fluttered in the breakfast room window; a teacup and saucer sat next to the sink on the otherwise spotless kitchen counter. Magazines, paperback books, and knitting materials were scattered around the living room, giving it a comfortable, lived-in look; the dark-paneled library, in contrast, was neat and slightly dusty, museumlike. *And it is a museum, sort of,* thought Elli sadly. It had been her deceased grandfather's favorite room. His chair, his desk. His books and model ships.

Elli stepped away from the library, the floorboards creaking under her feet. For a moment she stood still, the house's silence wrapping around her like a shroud. The cottage had been in her mother's family for generations; all at once, Elli saw it as old, sad, haunted. It had been nearly two years since her grandfather died, but the library still seemed echoing and empty without him. And

7

everywhere she turned, something reminded her of last summer. Last summer, and Laura.

Turning on her heel, Elli almost walked right into her brother. "Jeez, Ethan," she exclaimed in surprise.

"Sorry. What're you so jumpy for?"

She hugged herself, shivering. *It's like the house is full of ghosts,* she thought. Then she cleared her throat. "I was just feeling . . . I don't know. Edgy."

Ethan's eyes narrowed and his lips tightened in a thin line. "Don't talk about it," he warned. "I don't want to hear it. I won't listen."

"What? We're never supposed to speak her name again?" Elli shook her head. "This whole past year, and driving up here today, we've pretended that she never existed. Maybe *you've* forgotten her, Ethan, but I haven't."

A spasm of pain twisted her brother's handsome face. "I haven't forgotten her," he said hoarsely. "God, Elli. Do you really think there's a chance of that?"

He pushed past her, stomping into the kitchen. Elli returned to the front hall, retrieved her suitcases, and headed slowly upstairs.

Her bedroom door was ajar, but the door to the guest room next door was closed. *Who shut it?* she wondered. *Nana . . . or Ethan?* It was where Laura had slept the previous summer—another haunted room.

Her own room—the curtained dormer windows, twin beds with crisp white spreads, polished antique cherry furniture, old cedar toy chest—was sunny, familiar, and welcoming. With a sigh of relief, Elli dropped her bags and sank into the overstuffed easy chair. She was almost sorry now for what she'd just said to Ethan. *Of course he remembers Laura,* she thought. *Of course he's suffering.*

But a moment later her sympathy for her brother faded before the cold, simple facts. *Just minutes after Laura's death,* Elli recalled, *he was back in Charlotte's arms.* As if Laura had never even existed . . . and as if Charlotte herself weren't responsible for the fatal boating accident that dark late-summer night.

There wasn't a single place in the house where Ethan could escape the memories. He saw Laura sitting over her morning tea in the breakfast room, her long sandy-brown hair still sleep-tousled. He heard her in the kitchen chatting with his grandmother about the garden. She was curled up on the living room sofa with a book. She was sitting in one of the porch rockers, watching the sun set over the lake. And upstairs it was worse. Ethan stared at his bed, his breath coming fast and ragged. Was there a gentle depression in the pillows, the mattress, as if a slim form had been lying there just a moment before?

He pressed the heels of his hands against his eyes, obliterating the images. *Go away, Laura,* he pleaded silently. *Please, just leave me in peace.* He unpacked his duffels, hurling things haphazardly into the closet and dresser drawers. But Laura was still there—he saw her as she had been on their first day at Silver Beach the previous summer, laughing and playful, brimming with questions about the colony, with joy at the prospect of spending the whole vacation with him.

Ethan dropped onto the edge of his bed, resigned. *The counselor at school told me not to repress stuff,* he thought. *If I don't deal with it, if I don't face it, I'll never get past it.* So maybe this was the time and the place. Summer. Silver Beach. Where Laura McIver had drawn her last breath.

Ethan and Laura had dated for the last few months of sophomore year, and he'd invited her to spend the summer with him at his grandmother's cottage by the lake. They'd be counselors at the colony day camp—it would be romantic and fun, the best summer of their lives. Charlotte Ransom, Ethan's ex-girlfriend, hadn't seemed to pose a problem. Thanks to Laura, Ethan had finally gotten over his childish obsession with the girl who'd lied to him and cheated on him. Laura hadn't been the least bit worried about Ethan's old flame living right next door. She'd loved Ethan so much, and had been confident that he returned her love one hundred percent.

"And I did love her," Ethan whispered, a needle of pain piercing his heart. "But not enough."

How had it started? How had he gone from being over Charlotte to being obsessed with her once more? She'd been dating all those other guys, partying all night with a wild Pentwater crowd, and little by little, it had started to make him crazy. He had been concerned for her; he knew she was freaked out about Mr. Ransom and Mrs. Wells dating, and about the love letters Elli had found in the attic that proved the affair dated back to the time of Charlotte's mother's suicide. Then there had been the night of the Midsummer Madness costume ball, when everyone dressed like characters in an F. Scott Fitzgerald novel. *She wore a flapper dress just like Laura's,* Ethan remembered, *and walked up to me in the shadows and put her arms around me. We almost kissed.*

He'd resisted her then, resisted the unexpected surge of longing, the intense, bone-melting desire. He loved Laura—he was going to stay true to Laura. Until . . . the game.

Charlotte had suggested it—powerboat chicken in the cove after dark, a game they'd played as kids. *It was supposed to be just for fun,* Ethan thought, his hands clenching into fists. A silly dare, like the old days. He and Laura had taken one boat, while Charlotte, Sam, and Elli rode in the other. Charlotte and Ethan were driving.

His eyes blurred. Around him, the room grew

dark, almost as dark as that moonless August night. From opposite sides of the cove, he and Charlotte had gunned their engines, leaving their headlights off. He'd pointed his boat straight at hers, turning the throttle full force.

Ethan buried his head in his hands, asking himself the same question he'd asked a hundred, a thousand times before. "Why didn't I turn aside sooner?" he moaned. Because he'd thought Charlotte would laugh, call him a coward, like when they were young, when she'd won the game of powerboat chicken every time.

The nightmarish scene flashed through Ethan's mind. The two boats flying toward each other across the still black water; yanking the tiller at the last minute; both boats swerving, but not in time; the sickening crack of impact as Charlotte's boat drove into the side of his; the screams.

Laura's scream.

Laura, dead by the time Ethan pulled her body back to shore.

Rising, Ethan stalked to his bedroom window, flicking the shade all the way up. He stared across the south lawn at Briarwood, the Ransoms' cottage. There was a car in the driveway, a beach towel draped across the deck railing, and other signs of habitation, but he repressed the impulse to gallop right over. *She's not there,* he reminded himself. Ordinarily Charlotte was the first person back to Silver Beach, where her father lived year-round. But that spring she'd graduated from Bedford Hall and had flown off to Europe on vacation. *One more day,* Ethan thought. *One day without her.*

His throat tightened. All at once he was breathless and light-headed. He hadn't had a serious asthma attack in years, but now he could feel himself on the verge. *Cool it,* he told himself, backing up and sitting down on the bed. He closed his eyes and drew the air in slowly. Inhaler in hand, he waited for the threat of an attack to pass. When it did, he tossed the inhaler aside and hopped to his feet again. Once more he fixed his eyes on the house next door. He'd watch, and wait. And when she got there, everything would be okay. Charlotte wasn't a ghost—she was intensely, passionately *alive*. Ethan knew that she alone could make him forget what he'd done to Laura.

Elli found her grandmother by the water, sitting on a folding beach chair with a striped towel wrapped around her legs and a floppy straw hat on her head. "Catching some rays, Nana?" she called.

"Oh, you're here!" Eleanor Chapman stood up and held out her arms to embrace her granddaughter. "I didn't hear the car—must've been dozing."

They hugged tightly. "What a day," said Elli, smiling. "I may change into my suit and join you."

"Sometimes there's nothing like a little nap in the sun," Mrs. Chapman mused. "The sound of the waves on the shore, the birds, the breeze—it soothes the soul."

Elli glanced over her shoulder. She could see her brother on the porch of the house, pacing. Mrs. Chapman followed her gaze. "You're thinking Ethan could use some soul-soothing?" she guessed.

Elli nodded. "Look at him. He's so restless. He won't sit still until she gets here."

"He's still under her spell, then."

"Yep," Elli said briskly, then pushed the thought away. "Where's Mom?"

"She and Holling took out a canoe—going birding on Blueberry Island, I believe."

Elli sat down on the sand next to her grandmother's chair. "What do you think about them?" she asked. "It's getting serious, huh?"

"Appears to be."

"Him and Mom, Ethan and Charlotte. It's weird." Elli shook her head. "What *is* it about the Ransoms?"

Her grandmother smiled. "Walk back to the house with me," she said, leaving Elli's question unanswered. "It suddenly occurs to me that I skipped lunch, and I'm ravenous."

At the cottage, Mrs. Chapman greeted her grandson and then disappeared into the kitchen. Elli lingered on the porch with Ethan. "You're making me nervous," she teased. "Pacing like that—you look like some crazed maniac about to walk into a fast-food restaurant and start firing off an assault weapon."

Ethan didn't crack a smile. "Get off my case, Elli."

"I wasn't *on* your case," she retorted. "Sheesh, Ethan. Can't you take a joke?"

"No, because you're not joking," he shot back. "You're trying to get under my skin, like you always do."

"Well, maybe I am. Maybe I just wish you'd take a closer look at what you're doing." Elli glanced at Briarwood; she couldn't disguise her disapproval. "What you're doing with *her*."

"I love Charlotte," Ethan declared, his tone as cold and steady as his gaze. "And you'd better accept that, Elli. Or you and I—we can't be friends."

Before his sister could respond, the sound of car tires on gravel drifted over to them. A shiny red BMW rolled to a stop in the Ransoms' driveway. The driver's-side door swung open and a curvy girl with cascading honey-blond hair stepped out, her legs long and slim in faded jeans and cowboy boots. Charlotte, a day early.

Ethan shot down the porch steps and across the grass like an arrow. Elli turned her back on the reunion scene. As she stepped into the house her brother's words echoed in her head. *Accept it, Elli . . . or we can't be friends.*

Elli had always instinctively wanted to protect her brother from Charlotte Ransom. Could she accept their relationship now?

2

"How did it go at the clubhouse?" Mrs. Wells asked Elli the next day at lunchtime. She was standing at the kitchen counter, dicing celery for chicken salad. "Are you teaching sailing again this year?"

Elli grabbed a handful of grapes from the fruit bowl. "Actually, I decided to do something different. To stay fit, I'm going to train for the annual Midsummer Madness swim race to Blueberry Island. At the day camp, I'm taking over the little drama program Ethan and Laura launched last summer. Remember? The kids wrote and performed their own plays. It was a big hit."

"I remember," Mrs. Wells said quietly. "That's nice, honey."

"I mean, Ethan wasn't going to do it," said Elli, almost angrily. "He's back to teaching tennis with Charlotte."

Mrs. Wells sighed. "How about Sam?"

"He doesn't get here until later today," Elli replied. "And he's not going to be a camp counselor this summer, anyway. He's interning at the district attorney's office in Pentwater."

"A more serious summer job," Mrs. Wells remarked. "He'll be, what, a college senior?"

"Right," said Elli. "Yeah, it'll be great experience for him. I hope he'll have some spare time, though." She smiled. "For me. And did you hear about the work corps?"

Mrs. Wells shook her head as she ground fresh black pepper over the salad.

"It's to clean up the colony and fix things that were damaged in that big storm back in March," Elli explained. "The dock, the yacht club deck. And there are all those trees down, plus the debris on the beach. Lots of high-school and college-age kids are volunteering."

"Sounds like a good idea," said Mrs. Wells.

A few minutes later, they were sitting at the table with plates of chicken salad and tall glasses of iced tea. Elli leaned back in her seat, pleased that as far as her relationship with her mother was concerned, this summer was much better than the previous one. *Things were so awkward and tense last summer,* Elli remembered. *Mom and Dad weren't divorced yet, but she was seeing Mr. Ransom. Except she wouldn't admit she was seeing him—the whole colony was gossip-*

ing, but she kept insisting they were just good friends. And then when Elli was hunting in the attic for something to wear to the Midsummer Madness costume ball, she'd found the letters—love letters dating back to the summer when Elli and Charlotte were both eight years old, the summer Charlotte's mother took her own life.

At the end of the summer, when they were all still reeling from the shock of Laura's death, Mrs. Wells had announced that she wouldn't be returning to Winnetka with her kids—she planned to spend autumn in Silver Beach with her lover instead. *I hated her. I really hated her,* Elli recalled. *I didn't think I could respect her ever again.* But now they were . . . well, maybe not best friends, but mother and daughter again. Elli accepted the divorce and her mother's relationship with Mr. Ransom. Now that she was closer to being an adult herself, she was starting to understand that adults weren't perfect—they made mistakes, too.

Closer to being an adult. A pleasant shiver chased up Elli's spine. "Every time I think about September I totally get the chills, Mom," she said. "I'll be starting *college.* Can you believe it?"

Mrs. Wells smiled back somewhat wistfully. "I can, and I can't. Of course, I know you're ready, but time passes so fast. This is corny—what every mother says, right?—but it feels like it was just yesterday that you were a baby. Ethan and I will really miss you."

Elli felt an unexpected wave of emotion. There'd been so many times during the past few years when she'd wished she were older, already in college, living away from home so she didn't have to deal with the divorce, the family struggling to remake itself. And now she was older, and on her way to college—it was all happening so fast.

Leaning across the table, Elli put her hand over her mother's. "I'll miss you, too, Mom," she said, meaning it.

At noon Elli dismissed the campers in her drama group for the day, then stepped out of the yacht clubhouse to get some sunshine. She bumped into her brother and Charlotte, dressed in tennis whites.

"You two pick out a spot on the lawn," Ethan said once Elli had greeted the couple. "I'll grab some sandwiches and sodas at the snack bar and meet you back out here."

Elli opened her mouth to make an excuse, but Charlotte spoke first. "Yes, have lunch with us, Elli," Charlotte urged. "We haven't talked yet, and I want to hear *all* your news."

Ethan smiled at Elli, his expression hopeful, and she remembered his ultimatum. *Be nice to Charlotte, or else.* There was no graceful way to get out of it. "Sure," she mumbled.

As the two girls walked across the grass toward a cluster of birch trees, Elli kept looking over her shoulder in hopes of spotting some friends who might come to her rescue—Becky Nichols, Heather Courtland, Hugh Lowell, even the Madden twins, Amber and Amelia. Their catty gossip would have been preferable to a tête-à-tête with Charlotte. But no one else was around.

Make the best of it, Elli counseled herself as she dropped onto the lawn, sitting cross-legged.

Charlotte lay back, reclining full-length with her head pillowed on her arms. "You know, now that I'm not stuck living here year-round, I really get into Silver Beach," she said, tilting her face to the sun with a voluptuous sigh. "Don't you, Eleanor? Aren't you psyched to be back?"

Elli clenched her teeth. How could Charlotte be so bold, so relaxed, so carefree? It made Elli sick just to look at her. Charlotte was undeniably beautiful—her body slim and curvy, her face cat-like with its wide-set eyes and pointed chin, her glossy hair floating in golden waves on the grass. But her beauty was like a boast, a taunt. Elli couldn't see Charlotte without seeing another body, dragged from the water, lifeless; another lovely face, pale and still in death.

She looked away, stifling her emotions. "It is good to be back."

"And things between Briarwood and your cottage are going to be cozier than ever," Charlotte predicted, her mouth twisting with malicious amusement. "Now that Ethan and I are back together, and with your mom and my dad getting so *serious*."

Elli bristled. Charlotte had always disliked the thought of their parents dating even more than Elli herself did, and with good reason: Charlotte blamed the affair for her mother's death. *But that doesn't stop her from rubbing my nose in it,* Elli thought. *Anything to get under my skin.*

It had always been that way with her and Charlotte. When they were children, stuck playing together because they were next-door neighbors and the same age, Charlotte had always tried to dominate and bully Elli. When Elli wanted to make believe they were animals and zookeeper, Charlotte would insist on adding some violence. She wanted to be a hunter, shooting the animals. *And then she discovered the best game of all,* Elli thought bitterly. *Torturing Ethan. And she's still playing it.*

"I know you're not thrilled about me and Ethan," said Charlotte, as if reading Elli's mind.

"It's none of my business," Elli responded cautiously.

"But you're his big sister," Charlotte teased. "You've always taken such good care of him, and you don't think this is good for him. You don't think *I'm* good for him. Do you?"

Elli smiled tightly, determined to be civil for her brother's sake. "If Ethan's happy, I'm happy."

Charlotte laughed. "Saint Eleanor. You're so unselfish—it's really and truly too sweet. Well, don't you worry. Ethan *is* happy." She stretched her arms over her head, her top sliding up to reveal a sliver of slim, suntanned waist. "Wildly happy."

Elli really didn't want to hear the details. She knew her brother had lost his virginity to Charlotte two summers ago, and it was obvious that the sexual heat between them was more intense than ever. "What's taking him so long?" she wondered, glancing impatiently at the clubhouse.

"Probably ordered something hot from the grill—waiting for fries, or a burger," guessed Charlotte. "So what about *your* love life?" She sat up, leaning back on her hands, and gazed straight at Elli, her lake-blue eyes frankly curious. "You and Sam still hot and heavy?"

"We haven't seen each other in a month, but we're going out, if that's what you're asking."

"Yeah, that's what I'm asking. When's he going to show up?"

"Tomorrow, probably. Or maybe later today." *What's it to you?* Elli wanted to add.

"Good," said Charlotte, lying back down.

The question was still on the tip of Elli's tongue. *What's it to you?* She didn't ask it, though. Didn't need to—she knew the answer.

She wouldn't mind adding Sam to her list of

conquests. Charlotte had been turning the whole colony upside down and inside out for years. She'd dated every boy in northern Michigan. And the previous summer she'd caused Laura's death—whether by accident or on purpose—and stolen back Ethan's heart. No doubt about it: the world was wrapped around her little finger. But too much was never enough for her. Always, always, Charlotte Ransom wanted more.

Later that afternoon, Charlotte stood by the sliding glass door in the kitchen of Briarwood, eavesdropping with enjoyment on the scene taking place out on the deck.

"Ten days?" Grace Wells swept a hand through her shining blunt-cut hair. "And then you're back for two days and off again for a week?"

"Book tours, darling," Mr. Ransom explained dryly. "I haven't had much to say about the schedule. If you want to complain, call my agent."

"I'm not complaining," said Mrs. Wells, though her tone was still edged with disappointment. "It's just that this summer . . . it's supposed to be *our* time."

"And it will be." He reached for her. "But you have to understand. My writing—the book. It . . ." He shrugged, not finishing the statement.

Charlotte turned away, smothering a smile.

His writing—the book. Now you know what it feels like, Grace darling, she thought vindictively.

When Charlotte had arrived a few days earlier, her father had informed her that he'd be away for much of the summer promoting his new novel. She knew that when he *was* home, he'd spend most of his time secluded in his study, racked by the agony of early work on his next book. It was a devouring, never-ending cycle that had never left any room for his daughter. *And now it's going to sabotage his relationship with Mrs. Wells,* Charlotte anticipated as she grabbed a bottle of fruit-flavored seltzer from the fridge. *Serves her right. Serves them both right.* She twisted off the top and took a swig of seltzer, her eyes and heart hardening. Not that a rocky romance was punishment enough for what they'd done a decade earlier to Charlotte's mother.

An hour later, Mr. Ransom tossed a suitcase into the back of his car and drove off without saying good-bye to Charlotte.

And she didn't care. The moment the car was out of sight, she phoned Ethan. In a minute flat he was at her door, his green eyes shining with love and anticipation.

They pulled each other's clothes off as they hurried up the stairs to her bedroom. "This book tour is a great idea," Ethan murmured as he wrapped his arms around Charlotte, running his hands down her bare back, his lips on her jaw, her throat. "We get the house to ourselves."

They fell onto the bed, their limbs inter-twined. For a minute Charlotte just gazed at Ethan, admiring every inch of him, his lean, ath-letic body, the shaggy dark hair she loved to tan-gle her fingers in, his sea-green eyes, the chiseled yet sensuous features. Then she began teasing him with slow, lingering kisses, one after another. Finally Ethan moaned with impatience and reached over to pull the curtains.

"No," said Charlotte. "Leave them open. I like the light and the air."

"What if someone sees us?"

"What if?" she countered, playful and chal-lenging.

They made love as they always did, urgently, with abandon. "It's good, so good," Charlotte whispered to Ethan. And it was. He loved her madly, would do anything to please her, and she'd trained him well—he satisfied her more than any boy ever had.

When it was over, they lay quietly on the tousled sheets, their bodies bathed in the orange rays of the setting sun. As the shadows lengthened Ethan's eyelids drooped; a blissful smile on his face, he began to doze. Charlotte, though, was wakeful. Her eyes strayed to the window. Headlights sliced the dusk; a car pulled into the driveway of the Chapman cottage next door. She propped her-self up on one elbow to get a better view.

A guy, tall and well-built with dark chestnut hair, jumped out of the Mustang convertible and hurried toward the cottage. Elli was already running down the steps to meet him.

Sam DeWitt lifted Elli in his arms, swinging her in a circle. Charlotte frowned. She couldn't see their faces, but she could imagine the smiles, the laughter. Then Sam set Elli back on her feet, bending his head to hers. The two figures merged into one in a clinging, passionate kiss that went on and on.

Charlotte lay back on the cool pillows, her lips tightening in a resentful line. All at once, even though she'd just made love with Ethan, she felt hollow and unsatisfied. The one boy whose heart she'd never been able to capture was in the arms of Elli Wells.

Her mouth softened again, the lips parting as she whispered the name aloud. "Sam."

Ethan jerked awake. He turned to find Charlotte gazing at him, her eyes gleaming in the dark. "Guess I nodded off. Sorry," he mumbled sleepily.

"It's okay." She laughed. "Sex is no good if it doesn't tire you out, right?"

A cool evening breeze wafted through the window. Charlotte pressed her body against his, warming him. He brushed her cheek with a grateful kiss. "I love you, Char," he whispered.

She didn't reply with words, but her hand moved to his chest, her fingers rubbing in gentle, tantalizing circles. Her mouth found his and they were kissing again, quickly growing as excited as they'd been just an hour earlier.

Ethan let his mind go blank as he clung to her body, the only real thing in the world, the only thing that mattered. With Charlotte, it was just like Ethan knew it would be. He was able to lose himself completely, to forget everything and everyone else. Even the previous summer. Even Laura.

"It's so good to be back," Sam said to Elli the next morning as they strolled by the sparkling lake. "It was great having you visit me at school—I always wished you wouldn't leave." He squeezed her hand. "But for some reason, it's a hundred times better here."

"Silver Beach is our special place," Elli agreed.

They stopped walking and turned toward each other. Elli slipped her arms around Sam's waist, smiling up at him. Sam devoured her beautiful face with his eyes: the smooth, golden skin and classically sculpted features, the silky brown hair shining in the morning sun, the clear blue eyes, the inviting curve of her lips. "Elli Wells, I'm wild about you," he declared, bringing his mouth close to hers.

"I'm wild about you, too."

They kissed tenderly, then continued walking. "I always crack up thinking about it, though," Elli said, swinging his hand. "I mean, thinking about you and me. Like this. When I was a kid and you were my sailing instructor at day camp, I had such a crush on you! We all did—me, Heather, the twins, Margaret. I *wrote* about you in my *diary*."

Sam laughed. "Sorry I can't say the same, but you were kind of a runt back then. Tall, skinny, and flat as a board with that ponytail hanging all the way to your butt. It looked like you combed it out maybe once a month."

Elli giggled. "Twice a month."

"Then last summer." Sam whistled, remembering. "It was a whole other story. You didn't make it easy, but I figured I just had to be patient—a few years wasn't *too* huge an age difference. Now look at you—old enough to vote."

"Old enough to do a lot of things," she said meaningfully.

They kissed again, more passionately this time. Finally Elli drew away, laughing and blushing. "Whoa. Let's not forget we're in a public place."

Sam pulled her close again. "I've been apart from you for too long to get picky about where and when. So *when* I want to do this"—he nuzzled her neck, nibbled her earlobe—"I don't really care *where* we happen to be."

"I hate couples who make out in public, though," said Elli, lifting her face for another kiss.

"Me too," said Sam just before their lips met.

They walked the whole length of Silver Beach, rounding the tip of the peninsula by Sam's grandfather's mansion, Eagle Cottage, and finally stopping near the dock in the cove. The day campers hadn't arrived yet. Only one person stood on the beach, scratching his head as he studied an old wooden boat pulled up onto the sand.

"Hi, Mr. Emerson," Elli called out.

The old man turned to them, squinted to bring them into focus, then grinned. "Hello, kids," he boomed, his voice deep and gruff. "Nice morning, eh?"

"Good breeze," Sam commented. "Perfect for a sail. But it doesn't look like you'll be going anywhere in that."

The three stood looking at what was left of Mr. Emerson's beautiful old sailboat, the *Morning Mist*. The mast had been snapped in two, and there were gaping holes in the hull. "Yep, the storm last March got her good," Mr. Emerson said with regret. "My own fault—that's the worst of it. We were up for a weekend at Easter, had a real balmy day, so we took her out, then left her moored instead of putting her back in the shed. She broke free in the storm and slammed into the dock."

"Can't you fix her?" asked Elli.

"She's a work of art, made by hand by old Jim Cobb in Deep River back in forty-eight. But after that beating . . ." Mr. Emerson shook his head, his wrinkled face sorrowful. "She's fit only for scrap."

"Oh, no, you can't mean that!" Elli stretched out a protective hand toward the boat. "She's been in your family that long—you can't give her up."

"I don't have the energy to repair her," Mr. Emerson confessed, "nor the heart. No, it's time to say good-bye to the *Mist.*"

Sam looked from Elli to Mr. Emerson. Struck by a sudden inspiration, he spoke up. "Wait a minute, Mr. Emerson. What if you let us repair the boat?"

Elli nodded eagerly. "The *Mist* was always the prettiest boat in Silver Beach, and with some work, she could be again." Mr. Emerson looked skeptical. She placed a hand on his arm. "Oh, please, Mr. Emerson. Just give us a chance!"

"Don't want you wasting your time, that's all," he said. "Are you sure?"

"We want to do this," Sam said emphatically.

Slowly a smile creased the old man's face. "Then she's yours," he assented. "And I mean yours. If you get her floating again, it's only fair that she should belong to you."

They shook hands on it, and then Mr. Emerson headed back to Gull Cottage. Together, Elli and Sam contemplated *Morning Mist.* "It'll be

31

a big project," said Sam. "We're talking serious elbow grease here. Hours and hours of work."

"But just think of the reward at the end," said Elli, her eyes shining. "Anything worthwhile takes time and effort, right?"

They stood on the soft, sun-warmed sand, the water of the cove lapping gently near their feet. Sam put his arms around Elli and she leaned against him with a happy sigh. He felt a perfect peace wrap around his heart. There was a completeness to the moment; Silver Beach seemed to hold him the way he was holding Elli.

"Like us," Elli continued. "We had to work at this, at our relationship, but it's been fun work. And what we have together—I feel so lucky. We're not like Charlotte and Ethan. We don't play games, tell lies, keep secrets."

An unwelcome thought pushed into Sam's mind like a wisp of cloud crossing the sun. *Secrets,* he thought with a pang of guilt. *I wish I didn't know. Damn, why did he tell me?* But the fact was, he did know. The previous summer, his grandfather had revealed a devastating secret about Elli's family. Would Elli ever find out the truth? And if she did, what would it mean to her?

It was like being handed a bomb. He couldn't toss it—he couldn't tell Elli. It would only explode in their faces. So he had to go on holding it as it continued to tick.

3

"How come I never seem to get anywhere improving my serve?" Mrs. Wells asked Elli when they finished playing a set of tennis on the Silver Beach courts. "You aced me a couple of times and I didn't ace you once."

Elli watched her mother serve. "It's your toss," she concluded. "It's a little low, a little conservative. So when you make contact, your arm isn't fully extended, and the serve is a little flat. Watch." Elli took a ball from the pocket of her shorts and positioned herself behind the baseline. First she hit a low toss. Then she served again, this time tossing the ball high and straight. "See the difference?"

Someone else responded before her mother could. "Nice serve, Elli."

Elli turned. It was Charlotte, approaching from the far court with Ethan. "Hi, guys," said Elli.

"Looks like you're warmed up. What do you say we play some doubles?" suggested Charlotte, smiling across the net at Mrs. Wells.

Mrs. Wells shook her head. "Actually, we were just about to call it quits."

They'd intended to play another set, but Elli picked up on her mother's cue. "Another time," she agreed.

"I suppose you'll be playing more tennis and in general looking for things to do since my dad will be out of town so much this summer." Charlotte's smile was more like a smirk now. "If you ever want some tips, Mrs. Wells, just give a holler and I'll be happy to help you out."

"I'll do that, Charlotte," said Mrs. Wells, her own smile stiff.

Charlotte lifted her racket in a wave. "So long."

Elli and her mother watched the pair stroll off hand in hand. "I wish I could like that girl," Mrs. Wells declared when Ethan and Charlotte were out of earshot.

Elli shot a surprised look at her mother.

"Oh, honey, we don't have to pretend, do we?" Mrs. Wells asked, meeting Elli's eyes. "It's not just that she's fresh. That she's wild and un- reliable. She's— It's something deeper. She's been bad news ever since she was a baby. Whenever I see her and Ethan together . . . I'll never be happy about them dating. Never."

Elli had never heard her mother express her disapproval of Charlotte so explicitly. "Me either," said Elli as they stopped by the water fountain on their way off the court. "But you know what? There's nothing we can do about it. Ethan's chosen Charlotte. He's seventeen—he doesn't need our protection anymore."

Mrs. Wells looked at Elli thoughtfully. "You always did take good care of him, didn't you?"

Elli thought about their childhood, how she'd worried about her frail, asthmatic younger brother, putting herself in between him and the bigger kids who sought to bully and taunt him. *I could never keep him safe from Charlotte, though,* Elli mused, *especially when he went from gangly and awkward to hunky and gorgeous and she got interested in him in a whole new way.*

"The last couple of summers, I've wasted a lot of time stressing over Ethan and Charlotte," Elli confessed. "She's dangerous. And he loves her, so she has that much more power over him. That much more capacity to cause pain. But trying to tear Ethan away from Charlotte is like telling the sun to rise in the west and set in the east. It's not going to happen."

Mrs. Wells sighed. "You're right."

They walked down the gravel road toward their house. "I'm done worrying, done being afraid for him," Elli went on. "This is my last summer before college, and I want to enjoy it, you know?

I want to be happy every single minute."

"And I hope you will be." Mrs. Wells slipped an arm around Elli's waist and gave her a quick hug. "You deserve it, honey."

"We all deserve it, Mom," said Elli quietly. "You do, too. Are . . . are *you* happy? With Mr. Ransom?"

Mrs. Wells gazed into her daughter's eyes. "He can be moody," she admitted. "Distant, difficult. But we're— He's—" Her expression softened, grew dreamy. "He's an intellectual. A romantic. So different from—" She didn't say it, but Elli knew what she was thinking. *So different from Dad, the straitlaced, unromantic lawyer.* "Being with him opens up a whole new dimension of experience for me," Mrs. Wells added. "I discover a whole new side of myself. Yes, I'm happy."

Elli pondered her mother's words. *A whole new dimension of experience, a whole new side—is that what love is?* she wondered. *Is that what love does? For all of us—me, Mom, Ethan—in different ways?*

"This has been a perfect day," Elli said to Sam one Saturday afternoon as they worked on Mr. Emerson's old sailboat.

They'd spent a few hours in the morning helping with the colony rebuilding projects. Then, after Elli swam half a mile, they'd gone for a sail and picnicked by the eagles' nest on

36

Blueberry Island. Now her muscles felt loose and warm from exercise and sunshine.

"Any day I get to spend dawn to dusk with you is perfect," said Sam, using pliers to remove a jagged piece of wood from the boat's hull.

Elli laughed. "I like that. Keep talking."

"I miss you during the week," Sam told her, flinging the board onto a pile of scrap. "When I'm in Pentwater, at the office."

"But you like your job, don't you?"

"The job's great." Sam grinned. "I'm just afraid my boss is going to find out how much time I spend daydreaming. I'm supposed to be helping her get materials ready for a case—looking in books, photocopying stuff—and instead I'm staring into space thinking about you."

Elli blushed. "You don't really."

"Yeah, I do." He dropped the pliers on the grass and ran over to grab her. "I think about doing this," he murmured, squeezing her body close to his, "and this . . ."

They kissed, falling backward on the soft sand. Elli rolled away from Sam, laughing. "Look at the boat," she said, shaking her head. "Mr. Emerson's going to croak. It's like a skeleton."

Sam studied the hull. They had to remove all the damaged boards before replacing them with new ones. "It only *looks* like we're backpedaling," he told Elli. "We're making progress."

"I just don't know how we'll finish by the end

of summer," she said with a lazy sigh. "It's like building a whole boat from scratch."

"Things that are worthwhile take time," said Sam, gently tracing her jawline with his index finger. "Or so a very wise person I know once said."

Elli smiled at him. "I guess you have more patience than I do."

"That's how you get the big payoffs."

They lay back on the sand, Elli's head pillowed on Sam's shoulder. "So, what do you think about this law thing, now that you've been doing it for a week or two?" she asked.

"I like it. It's definitely what I want to do. Law school, and then maybe clerking with a judge."

"I can see you in one of those black robes yourself," Elli teased. "A Supreme Court justice."

Sam laughed. "Definitely. But it'll work out perfectly, don't you think?" He rolled onto his side, facing her. "I'll apply to law schools this year, and with some luck I'll get into someplace good that's not too far from you. I'll graduate from law school the same year you graduate from college."

Elli's eyes widened. It was the first time he'd spoken about the future to her. "You think about that? About down the road, you and me?"

"Don't you?"

She couldn't tell him she'd thought way beyond college and law school. Careers, kids, a house, a dog, summers in Silver Beach, and then someday two old people, still in love, rocking on the porch and watching the sun set over Lake Michigan. "Yeah, I think about it."

"I mean, what matters most is right here," said Sam. "Right now. But things are so good with you, Elli. And I'm pretty sure they'll just keep getting better."

He looked into her eyes with so much love and warmth, she felt dizzy with joy. "I still can't believe this is happening," she whispered. "How did I ever get so lucky?"

"We both got lucky," said Sam. "It was just meant to be."

Arms wrapped around each other, they lay gazing at the *Morning Mist*. All at once, Elli didn't see the boat as an old wreck, bare, brittle bones that might never again be something strong and whole. Instead, she saw the *Mist* reborn, the old and useless parts peeled away to reveal the new, the promise. The future. *It's like us. Our relationship,* thought Elli. *We've known each other forever—I've loved Sam DeWitt since I was a kid. This is old and new at the same time. It's the beginning.*

"We'll finish the boat before summer ends, and we'll sail it," Elli predicted. "Together."

"We will," Sam agreed, holding her tight.

"Hi, Mr. Ransom," said Elli as she mounted the porch steps.

Charlotte's father was sitting in what used to be Elli's grandfather's rocking chair, a cocktail glass in his hand. "Evening, Eleanor," he returned, his handsome face creasing in a smile. "And you know, you should really call me Holling. The other makes me feel so damned old."

"Holling," Elli repeated, smiling back at him to hide her discomfort. *Why, because you're dating my mother? Next thing I know, you're going to want me to call you Dad.* She pushed the thought from her mind. "Where's Mom?"

"Phoning the restaurant. She thinks we'll need a reservation since it's Saturday night."

"Well . . ." Elli drifted across the porch.

"Fix yourself a soda and come out and sit with us," Mr. Ransom invited. "We haven't talked in ages and I want to hear all about your plans for college."

Elli continued to edge toward the door. Most residents of Silver Beach considered Holling Ransom reclusive, antisocial, and eccentric, but ever since she was a little girl, Elli had been on friendly terms with him. He had given her books to read and had encouraged her childish scribblings. When she was older, she had helped him figure out how to use his new personal computer. *Every time I made the honor roll,* she recalled, *he was as proud as if I were his own kid.* Was that just because he was disappointed in Charlotte, a rebel always on the verge of flunking out of school? Or because of his feelings for

Elli's mother? *I'll bet that's it,* Elli thought. *He had something going with Mom, and being nice to me gave him an excuse to be close to her.*

"Thanks, but I— Actually, I have a date," said Elli, pulling open the door. "I'd better start getting ready." She waved good-bye and slipped into the house.

"Have fun," Mr. Ransom called after her.

When her mother and Mr. Ransom had finished their cocktails and driven off in his Mercedes, Elli wandered back out to the porch. She didn't really have a date, although she and Sam would meet up later for a walk in the moonlight, as they did every night. *And Ethan's off with Charlotte. Wonder what Nana wants to do for dinner?*

Her grandmother wasn't in the house, nor in the dusky garden. Elli scanned the beach. The sun had just set and the sky was still streaked with red and purple. Elli could barely make out the silhouettes of two people walking along the water. Both were white-haired; the woman was petite and erect, the man tall and lean with slightly stooped shoulders. *Nana and Mr. DeWitt,* Elli said to herself.

The pair moved slowly northward. At the edge of the Chapmans' beach, Mrs. Chapman stopped. Elli watched curiously as they lingered, still talking. Then Mr. DeWitt bent toward Mrs. Chapman, and she moved closer to him. Did they kiss?

41

Elli couldn't be sure—the twilight had descended, obscuring the scene with shadows. *No,* she decided. *I must have been imagining things. Nana and Mr. DeWitt, making out on the beach?* Laughing to herself, she rocked quietly in her grandfather's chair.

A few minutes later, Mrs. Chapman came back down the beach and took the path through the dune grass across the lawn. When she saw Elli on the porch, she lifted her hand in a wave of greeting. "Aren't the mosquitoes eating you alive, dear?"

"I'm coated with bug spray," Elli assured her.

Mrs. Chapman lowered herself into the other rocker and pulled her cardigan sweater close. "Don't know why I get so chilled—it's a warm enough night. Old bones, I guess. Thin blood."

Elli laughed. "You're not old, Nana. You looked about sixteen out there, walking in the sand."

Her grandmother smiled. "I still feel sixteen inside. That's the funny thing about aging. It only happens to your body, not to your heart. Sometimes I look in the mirror and I actually gasp. 'Who's that old lady?' I wonder."

Elli grinned, then gestured toward the beach. "You were hanging out with Mr. DeWitt?"

"We took a bird-watching walk. That man's eyes are as sharp as ever, I'll grant him that."

Elli tucked her feet up on the rocker, wrapping her arms around her knees. "You two are . . . special friends."

42

"We go back absolutely centuries," Mrs. Chapman affirmed.

"And since Grandpa died . . . I mean, he's a widower, too."

Mrs. Chapman was thoughtfully silent for a moment. Then she nodded. "Yes, we're both alone. Of course, poor Mavis, Ted's wife, has been gone for years. But yes. We have our gardens, our card games, our bird walks." Her eyes twinkled at Elli in the dark. "And we gossip about our grandchildren. It passes the time."

"I didn't mean to pry," said Elli.

"You weren't. Don't worry, my dear." Mrs. Chapman rose to her feet. "Now, supper. How about I heat up a couple of those tasty French-bread pizzas?"

"Fine with me," said Elli.

At ten o'clock, after dinner and some television with her grandmother, Elli slipped out of the house. Cutting over to the shore, she walked quickly up the beach the way Mr. DeWitt had walked a few hours earlier. Past Gull Cottage, and past the Lowell, Fisher, Fairleigh, Gamble, and Madden houses. Then, at the end of the peninsula, through a stand of tall white pines, she glimpsed a wide lawn bright in the moonlight and the largest cottage in the colony, Theodore DeWitt's majestic Eagle Cottage.

Sam was just descending the steps of the three-story, cupola-topped white mansion. "Who goes there?" he called softly when he spotted her.

"A trespasser, and I'm up to no good," Elli announced. "I'm after the body of the young man of the house."

Sam grabbed her around the shoulders, pretending to tackle her. "Better defend myself, then," he grunted. "Nobody takes advantage of the DeWitts. Hey, wait a minute. What am I saying? Take advantage of me, please."

Laughing, they strolled back toward the lake with their arms around each other. "Warm enough for a swim, do you think?" asked Elli.

"When isn't it?"

Late-night swims had been a ritual starting two summers earlier, when Elli and Sam were teaching sailing together at the day camp. *One of the most precious parts of a Silver Beach summer,* Elli thought with a happy sigh. And better than ever now that she and Sam were a couple.

At the edge of the water, they stopped. Sam tossed off his T-shirt and waded into the lake up to his ankles. Elli stripped off her T-shirt and shorts and stood for a moment in her bathing suit. Then she glanced at Sam. After a moment's hesitation, she quickly slipped out of her bathing suit and raced into the water naked. She dove, stroking out to deeper water.

"I think I'm hallucinating," Sam said, splashing after her. "I just saw this incredible vision. It couldn't have been Elli Wells, though. She's too shy to skinny-dip."

Elli laughed, enjoying the delicious feeling of silky, cool water against her warm, bare skin. "We used to sneak out of the house and do this all the time, me and Ethan and Sally Hammond, when we were kids," she reminded Sam. "You caught us that time, remember?"

"Yeah, but that was before you, shall we say, blossomed. There wasn't a whole lot to see."

"Well, it feels great," she told him. "You should get rid of those trunks."

"Is that a proposition?"

She grinned. "You bet."

They were in shoulder-deep water. Elli paddled closer to Sam and he reached for her, wrapping his arms around her and pulling her into the shallows. The water was up to their waists now, and they kissed passionately, their wet bodies pressed close together.

Elli's blood was heating up, her heart pumping faster. She could feel Sam's desire for her increase, his urgency matching her own. "Let's go get that beach blanket," she whispered, her lips at his ear.

Sam took a deep, shaky breath. He held her at arm's length, averting his eyes. "Elli, I think you'd better . . . Put that suit back on, would you?"

"Why?" she asked.

Sam waded to shore, Elli at his heels.

Grabbing the beach blanket, he folded it around her. "You're too beautiful," he told her. "Too tempting. I don't trust myself."

"But *I* trust you. I . . . I love you," she added breathlessly, saying it out loud for the first time.

Sam placed his hands on either side of her face. "God, Elli. I love you, too," he said, his voice rough with emotion. "So much."

She placed one of her hands over his, grasping his fingers tightly. Then she led him to the dune, and they sat side by side in the grass. "If we feel that way, if we're both committed to this relationship, then it's okay," she said. "I'm ready, Sam. I want to."

"It's not just about wanting to. I've wanted to since—" He shook his head, laughing. "Well, never mind since when. I want you, Elli, like crazy. But sex is a big step."

"I'm not a child," she pointed out. "I'm eighteen. And I have birth control, if that's what you're worried about."

He looked surprised. "Where, in your shorts pocket?"

She giggled. "Back at the house."

"Lot of good it's doing us there."

"It'll only take me a minute to run back and—"

Sam put a finger to her lips. "Listen, Elli. I still think we should wait. What's happening to us is so incredible. I want us to take our time, every step of the way." He gazed into her eyes, his own eyes glowing. "And tonight . . . tonight you told me you love me. That's all I need right now. That's blowing my mind as it is."

Elli was suddenly on the verge of tears. Tears of pure happiness, of amazement that anybody could be as wonderful as Sam. "I do love you," she whispered. She said it again, with heartfelt conviction. "I love you, Sam DeWitt."

"I love you, too, Eleanor Wells," he replied, stroking her damp hair. "I love you, I love you, I love you . . ."

They were both still whispering the words when their lips met in the sweetest, gentlest kiss they'd ever shared.

"They weren't talking about what I *think* they were talking about. Were they?" asked Ethan as he and Charlotte stood on the porch of Briarwood, saying good night.

They'd been watching a video when Mr. Ransom and Mrs. Wells returned from dinner at the Golden Dunes Café in Pentwater. Their parents had passed by the den, deep in conversation, and Ethan and Charlotte had caught a few words. "God, I hope not," said Charlotte. "There's something deadly about that phrase, 'the future.' I hate it."

"It would be pretty weird if they got married," Ethan agreed, "but it wouldn't have to mean we couldn't . . . I mean, it wouldn't make us *related*."

47

He moved to kiss her, but Charlotte twisted from his arms. For some reason, seeing her father with Mrs. Wells had poisoned her mood more than usual that evening. "Ethan, I'm really tired," she mumbled. "Why don't you just . . . I'll see you tomorrow, okay?"

He stepped back from her, surprise and disappointment in his eyes. "Can't I come upstairs, for just a few minutes?"

"I'll see you tomorrow," she repeated. She brushed his lips with a kiss. " 'Night."

" 'Night, Char," he said, gazing into her eyes. "I love you."

"I love you, too," she said.

He started across the dark lawn. Halfway home, he turned to look back at her. Charlotte lifted her hand, blew him a kiss. When she heard his porch door slam, she darted down the steps, striding toward the beach.

She'd been lying to Ethan—she wasn't the least bit tired. But she also wasn't in the mood for fooling around with him, for assuring him over and over that yes, she loved him, with all her heart and soul. She wanted to be alone. She wanted everyone else in Silver Beach to just disappear.

She walked up the beach at the water's edge, the tiny waves lapping her bare feet and dampening the hem of her long, gauzy skirt. The row of cottages was dark; the colony went to sleep early. Only the lights of Eagle Cottage twinkled through the trees. *Sam,* thought Charlotte, her pulse quickening. *He's still up.* Maybe she could talk him into a walk, a few beers.

Then she saw the two figures emerging from the lake. The boy wrapped a blanket around the girl as they retreated to the shelter of the dunes.

Charlotte spun on her heel, her eyes smarting. *Damn you, Elli Wells,* she thought as she raced back down the beach, her hair flying in the wind. *Why should you get him? Why should you always get everything?*

Elli, Elli, Elli. Charlotte chanted the name in her head, hating it more with every repetition. She could almost hate Sam, too, for wanting Elli instead of her. Almost, but not quite. She wanted him too much.

Charlotte shivered with bitter rage at the thought of what Elli and Sam were doing, in the dark, in the dunes. But that thought wasn't all that tormented her. She and Ethan had sex— great sex. *Why isn't it enough?* she wondered.

The truth flashed through her brain, as bright and brief as a flicker of heat lightning. *Because Elli and Sam are in love, and Ethan loves me but I don't love him. I can't love him. I'll never be able to love anybody.* Charlotte shoved the horrible thought back under the surface. She ran faster, her toes digging into the sand. *Love.* Her father loved Mrs. Wells. Had for years. And now they were discussing the future.

Charlotte stopped dead. Her hair fell in damp curls about her face; her arms dangled limply at her sides. She stood, panting. Hatred boiled up in her again, but not for Elli this time—for Elli's mother. Hatred . . . and fear. *They can't marry,* Charlotte thought desperately. *They can't. They won't.* But she couldn't calm herself. Her heart pounded harder and harder, battering inside her chest. How much more could she take before she exploded?

4

A gentle evening rain tapped against the windows of Elli's bedroom. She thumbed through the stack of new paperback books on her nightstand, choosing a spy thriller. Then she went over to her portable radio–compact disc player. "Where's that CD?" she mumbled, pushing the flat plastic cases around in search of the music she felt like listening to. She raised her voice, loud enough to carry through her half-open door and down the hall. "Ethan! Did you steal my new Coldplay?"

A minute later her brother padded into her room in tube socks and gym shorts. He tossed the compact disc on her bed, grinning. "Sorry. But when I came in here to borrow this I found, like, ten of *my* CDs. You're a total klepto."

Elli laughed. "Am not."

"Are too."

She put on Coldplay, adjusting the volume. Her

brother dropped onto her bed, and Elli folded herself into the easy chair. "It's a good night for curling up with a cup of hot chocolate and a trashy novel," she observed.

Ethan nodded. "I was planning on writing some postcards. Haven't written to Gram and Gramps Wells in ages."

"Me either," said Elli. "We haven't seen them in ages, either. Funny, isn't it? We always knew Nana and Grandpa so much better. Because of our summers here, I guess."

"So what do you think's going on between Nana and Mr. DeWitt?" asked Ethan.

Elli raised her eyebrows. "You've noticed, too?"

"Hard not to. They're together all the time."

"They just like the same things. Gardening, birds, playing cards. I bet they talk about their stock portfolios, stuff like that. I mean, they're *old*."

Ethan stuck his arms behind his head, smiling up at the ceiling. "But not necessarily too old to—"

"Ethan!" Elli exclaimed with a shocked giggle. "We're talking about Nana."

"Okay, forget Nana. We know Mom and Mr. Ransom—"

Elli rolled her eyes. "Yeah, we know about *them*."

"It's pretty intense."

"I'll say."

"Char and I heard them talking the other night,"

Ethan went on. "About the future. Charlotte freaked out about it. Me, I don't particularly care what they do, but she really doesn't want them to get married."

At the thought of her mother marrying Mr. Ransom, Elli felt a sickening twinge in her gut. Sometimes she and Charlotte were more alike than she wanted to admit. "I wouldn't be wild about the idea, either," she confessed.

"How come?" Ethan asked. "What difference would it make to us? I mean, you're going to college—you'll never live at home again, probably. She's bound to remarry someday. Dad too."

"Yeah, but . . ." Elli just couldn't explain it. Was it because of the past? *If Mom married Mr. Ransom, we'd all be living with it for the rest of our lives. What they did to Mrs. Ransom ten years ago. And Charlotte would be my stepsister. Ugh!* "Forget it. Let's not talk about it."

"Okay." Ethan gave Elli's pillow a light punch. "Hey, I've been wanting to tell you," he said after a moment. "I'm—I'm psyched for you and Sam. You guys are a great couple. You seem really happy."

Elli smiled brightly. She knew she looked like an idiot, but she didn't care. "We *are* happy. Oh, Ethan, I just can't tell you! I've never felt like this about anybody in my whole life. Nothing's even come close. We're talking *major* chemistry." Her face turned pink. "But that's not all there is to it.

The best part is that we're best friends. We just have so much fun together, and we can talk about absolutely everything." She laughed. "I'm totally babbling. I guess it's just—"

She broke off, startled by the sad shadow in her brother's eyes. "What is it, Ethan?" she asked, puzzled. "Isn't that how you've always felt about Charlotte?"

"Yeah. I suppose so," Ethan mumbled, averting his eyes. He rose to his feet and headed to the door.

Elli followed him to his room. "Do you want to talk about anything?" she asked softly.

Ethan went straight to the window. He pulled the shade, then let it snap up again. Looking over his shoulder, Elli could see the candle glowing in Charlotte's bedroom window across the way. It was their old signal.

"No. I've got to go." His words were muffled as he pulled a sweatshirt over his head. Sticking his feet into a pair of flip-flops, he breezed past Elli into the hallway. "See ya."

"'Night," she said.

Elli continued to ponder the flickering candle as Ethan's feet pounded down the stairs. Why did Ethan seem so troubled? He had what he'd always wanted more than anything, didn't he?

Ethan lay in Charlotte's bed, listening to her quiet, even breathing. Usually he was the one who fell asleep first, but that night he was wide awake and restless while she sighed in her dreams, her arms around him and her head tucked under his chin.

Charlotte, wake up, he wanted to say. *Wake up—we need to talk.* But he didn't speak, didn't move. What would they talk about, anyway? Their relationship? The future—the concept Charlotte had reacted so strongly against when they heard their parents discussing it? She'd only laugh. "Who needs the future when we have right now?" she'd say, tickling him. "Isn't . . . *this* . . . enough for you, Ethan Wells?"

No, she wouldn't want to talk about it. It would be like when he'd brought up the subject of his college interviews and applications, just that evening. Should he apply to the school where she'd be a freshman in the fall? He wasn't pushing any kind of commitment on her—he just wanted to know. Did she want him to make that an option for them?

Charlotte had brushed aside the topic like a pesky mosquito. In a few seconds, she had his clothes off and he was too busy kissing her to think about anything else. And as always, being with her was mind-blowing. The connection between them, both emotional and physical, was stronger all the time. It almost hurt, almost made him want to cry out. She meant so much to him— he couldn't imagine his life without her in it.

Ethan stroked Charlotte's hair, lightly so as not to wake her. He touched her face ever so softly, as if to prove to himself that she was real, solid, there. No, he couldn't imagine life without her, but at the same time, Ethan suddenly realized that despite all his talk about college applications he couldn't really picture a future *with* Charlotte, either. He couldn't picture them planning together, the give-and-take, the everydayness of a steady long-term relationship. He couldn't picture them settling down. Charlotte, settling down?

He remembered the way Elli had described her relationship with Sam. *Best friends, able to talk about everything.* What appealed to him was the comfort level, the security. *It's not like that with Charlotte,* thought Ethan. With Charlotte, it was like spinning around in outer space. No gravity, no lifeline. Glorious and hopeless at the same time. But it was a feeling he just had to have. He was addicted. As soon as they were apart the need kicked in again, fiercer than ever.

Go home, Ethan told himself. *Get some distance. Sleep in your own bed.* He tensed his muscles, preparing to slide away from Charlotte, to leave her. Then his body relaxed again. He couldn't do it. Her arms were locked around his waist; even in sleep, her hold on him was complete. He wouldn't leave until she sent him away.

* * *

Sam was in the kitchen the next night, rummaging through the refrigerator, when he heard the knock on the front door. "Come in!" he shouted.

He expected one of his guy friends—Forrest or Tim or Chip. Instead, when he turned around, a slice of cold pizza in his hand, he saw Charlotte standing in the doorway. "Char," he said in surprise. "What's up?"

"Nothing," she replied, leaning against the door frame with a smile. "And I happen to know that nothing's up with you, either, because Elli and Ethan are taking their grandmother out for dinner."

"Yep, I'm off duty," Sam kidded.

"So let's do something," Charlotte suggested, her eyes sparkling playfully.

Sam was cautious. "Like what?"

She laughed. "Don't panic. I'm not going to try to seduce you. I just feel like taking a drive, getting a beer somewhere."

Sam relaxed somewhat. It would be a relief to think he and Charlotte were at a point where they could joke about this. *We're both seeing other people,* he thought. *She's not going to throw herself at me like she does every summer. We're past that.* "Yeah, sure. I'm up for getting out of the house. I'll grab my keys."

It was a beautiful summer night. When they left Silver Beach's gravel road and hit the asphalt,

Sam hit the gas and the convertible shot forward, its engine purring powerfully. Charlotte shook her hair in the breeze. "So, you're going to be a senior this year," she remarked. "Next summer you'll be a college grad—you'll have a real job somewhere, a real life. Don't suppose you'll come back to Silver Beach."

"Just for a weekend now and then."

"I'm so psyched for college." Charlotte scanned Sam's CD collection, then stuck one in the deck. "I'm definitely going to look for something else to do during the summer from now on—work in the city, travel. Forget Silver Beach."

"What about Ethan?" asked Sam.

"What about him?" Charlotte asked, a playful note in her voice.

Sam shrugged, feeling too carefree, too entranced by the moonlit meadow they were driving past, to dig any deeper.

After a minute, Charlotte twisted in the seat, contemplating Sam's profile. "What do you think about me and him, anyway?"

"Don't know." Sam tapped the palm of his hand against the steering wheel. "I guess I think . . . you've dated around. You know what you want. Last summer, even with Laura here, you went after him. You two seem pretty steady at this point. He's the one you've picked."

Charlotte laughed, but it was a humorless

sound. "Yeah, and what great pickings, huh? Northern Michigan—this is really prime territory. Local yokels and the Silver Beach preppy bores."

Sam frowned. He was starting to wish he'd turned Charlotte down and stayed home with the TV and cold pizza. "Where did you want to go?" he asked her. "Deep River? Pentwater?"

"Oh, I really don't— Look!" Charlotte cried out suddenly. "Oh, stop the car, Sam. See the deer?"

He hit the brakes. Just to the side of the deserted back road, some deer were peacefully grazing. "Pull over," Charlotte commanded. "Turn off the engine. I want to look at them."

Obediently Sam steered the car onto the shoulder. He killed the engine and the lights. Charlotte rolled her window all the way down and leaned out. "Aren't they beautiful?" she breathed.

"Two does and three fawns," Sam said, smiling. "Somebody had twins."

They sat quietly for a few moments, gazing at the sight. Then Charlotte turned away from the deer. She leaned close to Sam, her hand on his knee and her long, soft hair tumbling forward. "Sam," she whispered.

Sam's spine stiffened. When Charlotte's hand slipped up his thigh, he grasped her wrist. "Cut it out, Char."

"Don't be such a wet blanket," she teased, leaning even closer. Her breasts brushed his arm. "Why shouldn't we have a little fun? Elli doesn't have to find out."

Sam pushed her back against her seat. "Damn, Char, why do you always make me do this?" he asked gruffly. "Why can't we ever just—"

He broke off, seeing her blank stare. He knew she didn't understand that he just didn't want her. She'd always been able to wrap every other guy she knew around her little finger. She'd had them all on their knees, begging, since she was eleven or twelve.

"That's what *I* want to know," she said petulantly. "Why can't we ever just . . . just once? Why won't you give me a chance? We'd be great together, I know it. Better than you and Elli. Better than me and—"

"Because I don't want to, Charlotte," Sam cut in. "I've never wanted to. I've never been interested in you that way and I never will be. I'm sorry to have to say that, but I don't know how else to get the message across."

Charlotte drew back, her eyes hooded. Her face twisted with fury. As quick as a snake, she whipped her arm through the air and slapped his face. "You—you—" she sputtered. "You don't know what's going on with me. You don't know what you're doing, what a mistake you're making."

Before he could stop her, she'd opened the passenger-side door and scrambled out of the car. "Char, where are you going?" He yanked on his own door handle, preparing to follow her. She couldn't walk home from there; they were miles from Silver Beach.

But Charlotte was already running down the road. Headlights approached—a pickup truck. Charlotte stuck out her arm, thumb pointing up.

"Char, let me take you home!" Sam shouted.

The pickup slowed. The driver, a twenty-something local with a five o'clock shadow, peered out the window, eyeing Charlotte from head to toe. Then he leaned across the seat, pushing the passenger-side door open for her. Charlotte climbed in without another look back at Sam. The truck took off, tires screeching.

Sam sighed heavily. He leaned back against his car, watching the truck's taillights until they disappeared. "Damn," he muttered. "Damn."

It was pretty much an annual ritual with him and Charlotte. She put the moves on him, he resisted. He'd pissed her off in the past, but never like this. He'd never seen her so enraged. *She's on the edge, and when she gets crazy, when she's thwarted, when she's this mad, she could do anything.* He thought about Laura McIver, the fatal game of powerboat chicken, and a shudder ran through him. He'd always insisted to Elli that Laura's death had been an accident, but he couldn't deny that Charlotte had set it up to happen. Sam knew only too well the damage Charlotte was capable of doing. What would she do now?

5

"We're going to need a bunch more wood screws," Elli told Sam as she ran a hand over the *Morning Mist's* bow. "And I'm ready to start sanding this part. Do you have any sandpaper back at the cottage, or should I rummage around the basement at my house?"

"We probably have some," Sam replied. He stood at the stern, pulling an old nail out with the claw of a hammer. "Give me a minute and I'll run and get it."

For a while longer they worked together on Mr. Emerson's old boat in companionable silence, humming along to the portable radio that was propped up on a toolbox. The late-afternoon sun beat warmly on Elli's bare shoulders and she felt contented and peaceful.

"So you really think you're going to salvage this old wreck?" a lilting voice called from behind them.

Elli and Sam both turned. Charlotte sauntered toward them, wearing a bikini top and very short denim cutoffs. "I mean, all the time you're putting into it," Charlotte continued. "Why not just buy a new boat?" The corner of her lip lifted in a disdainful smile. "Or are you that hard up for things to do?"

Elli saw Sam flinch. She didn't appreciate Charlotte's snide comments, either, but nothing could spoil her mood. "We're having fun," Elli reported cheerfully. "Sure, it's a lot of work, but when it's done, this boat is going to be beautiful again. They don't make 'em like this anymore, right, Sam?"

Sam had turned his back to Charlotte and was attacking another rusty old nail with a vengeance. "Uh, yeah," he grunted.

"I can just *hear* your enthusiasm," Charlotte said to Sam. "Well, different strokes for different folks, I guess. Later, kids."

She walked on past them toward the boathouse. When she was out of earshot, Elli shook her head, laughing. "Good ol' Char, always such a ray of sunshine. I really don't know what my brother sees in her."

"Mm-hmm," Sam mumbled.

"I mean, I know what he *sees* in her. But she's such a—" Elli laughed wryly. "Then again, I suppose she acts differently around guys she's trying to impress. Ethan thinks she's an angel."

Sam mumbled something else incoherent. Elli tilted her head to one side. "You seem bummed," she commented.

"She just . . ." Sam swiped at a nail with the hammer. "She's a pain."

"Don't let her get to you," Elli advised.

"She doesn't get to me," Sam said quickly.

"Well, she used to get to me. But I've decided there's no point worrying about Ethan. The worst thing she can do is break up with him, and that would be the best thing in the long run." Elli walked around the boat to stand next to Sam. "I just feel really lucky," she said softly, slipping her arms around his waist. "Char's the way she is because she's unhappy. And I have you." Sam set down the hammer and hugged her close. She smiled playfully up at him. "I'd be jealous of me, too."

"You *do* have me," he confirmed, his voice husky. "So don't ever let go."

"I won't," Elli promised.

At sunset Charlotte wandered restlessly down the beach. She knew Ethan was waiting for her—they had plans to meet at his house and then drive into the village for pizza and a movie. But she didn't want him to see her in this frame of mind. It wasn't just that she was feeling irritable—sometimes it was fun to be moody around him, to get him worried that she was mad at him for some reason. That day, though, she was beyond irritable. The anger boiling just under the surface had a new quality about it. It was stronger and less focused; she couldn't grasp it, didn't know how to use it. She was afraid of it.

Uppermost in her thoughts was the scene the night before with Sam. *How dare he,* she thought. No one had ever spoken to her like that, so bluntly, so *dismissively.* How had he put it? "I've never been interested in you and I never will be." *He doesn't want me—he wants Elli Wells.* Charlotte stomped through the tall, prickly dune grass. *Stupid Elli Wells, who was valedictorian of her stupid high school class and is going to some fancy college in the fall. Stupid Elli, with all her stupid sailing and tennis trophies. And her goody-goody personality—everybody's damned best friend. Stupid, adorable Elli Wells. Well, Sam DeWitt, I don't want you, either!*

Charlotte walked quickly along the gravel road toward the Chapman cottage. Reaching the driveway, she cut around the side of the house, expecting to find Ethan waiting impatiently on the porch. Only one person was in sight, however: Grace Wells, in the garden.

If there was anyone Charlotte hated more than Elli, it was Elli's mother. But Elli's mother was also Ethan's mother. "Good evening, Mrs. Wells," Charlotte called, her voice silky and sweet. "Wow, your roses look fantastic this year."

"Don't they?" Mrs. Wells straightened her back and gazed at a rosebush laden with deep-red blooms. "But I can't take any credit for them. My mother's the one with the green thumb."

Charlotte rested her arms on top of the fence. "The vegetables are yours, though, aren't they? I see you in here weeding and watering all the time."

"It's hard to go wrong with zucchini and green beans and tomatoes and squash." Mrs. Wells brushed some dirt from her hands, then bent to pick up the roses she'd cut. "I'll give you some of these to take home with you, Charlotte. Some for your room and some for your father's study."

Charlotte held the gate open for Mrs. Wells. "How sweet of you," she said, unable to keep an edge of sarcasm from her voice. "That would be just delightful."

Mrs. Wells looked at her with the same detached, speculative expression she'd directed at the rosebushes a minute earlier. "I suppose you're here to see Ethan," she said, her voice distinctly cooler than it had been a moment before.

"Of course." Charlotte looked Mrs. Wells straight in the eye and smiled, relishing the dislike and distrust she saw there. *She hates me going out with her precious son,* thought Charlotte. *She's never liked it one bit. Well, how does she think I feel about her going out with my precious dad?* "And we'll probably be out late." Her tone was teasing, flippant, fresh. "Don't wait up."

Mrs. Wells opened her mouth, as if about to say something. Then she pressed her lips together. *Her perfectly made-up lips,* Charlotte noted. *Just the right shade of red. And gardening in linen trousers and a silk top. Classy, classy Grace Chapman Wells. Grace Chapman Wells Ransom?*

"Have a nice evening," Mrs. Wells said, breezing past Charlotte without inviting her inside.

It didn't matter—Ethan was at the door and on his way out. Charlotte, however, was hardly aware of him. Her eyes remained fixed on Mrs. Wells as she climbed the porch steps, her arms laden with roses. So perfect, so sophisticated. And cultured and well-read—she and Mr. Ransom were always talking about boring books and opera and arty films. *So different from Mom,* thought Charlotte, her throat tightening. *Mom didn't go to college. She read trashy romance novels, not the kind of literary fiction Dad writes. She never hung out in Silver Beach wearing linen and silk, perfume and lipstick.*

"Ready?" asked Ethan, taking her hand.

Charlotte nodded. Yes, she was ready. She was ready to revenge herself on Sam and Elli, and on Mrs. Wells. On Mrs. Wells especially: Mrs. Wells, who'd stolen so much from her. *Mom's life, and Dad's love and attention. Well, it's my turn now, Grace,* Charlotte thought. *My turn to steal something back from you. But what?*

She turned to Ethan. He was looking at her, the usual hopeful, expectant, devoted expression in his green eyes. *Of course.* Slowly a smile spread across Charlotte's face. *She hates me having him, taking him away from her,* Charlotte thought. *She can't wait to get rid of me—she can't wait for us to outgrow this relationship. But what if we don't? What if I make sure Ethan belongs to me forever?*

The movie was a slapstick comedy, but Charlotte didn't laugh once. They ordered her favorite pizza, pesto and sun-dried tomato; she ate only half a slice. "Don't you feel well, Char?" Ethan asked solicitously as they walked back to his car.

"I feel fine," Charlotte replied, but her tone was uncharacteristically subdued.

On the way home, he stopped at a state park, one of the prettiest beaches around and their favorite after-dark spot. "It's a warm night. Let's take a walk," Ethan suggested.

Charlotte hunched her slender shoulders. "Maybe I am kind of tired," she said, turning her face away from him to look out the window. "Do you mind just taking me home?"

"No, I don't mind." Ethan reached for the key in the ignition to start the engine again, his hand suddenly shaking. "If that's what you want."

He drove toward Silver Beach, his head

spinning as he pondered the possible reasons for Charlotte's strangely quiet mood. *She's going to break up with me,* he thought with dread. *There's some other guy, like Sloan Hammond two summers ago. Oh, God, I should've known this couldn't last.*

By the time he pulled into her driveway, the panic had tensed his whole body—he could barely get out of the car to open the door for Charlotte. She didn't seem to notice his distress, however. She walked slowly toward Briarwood, her eyes downcast.

On the porch steps, Ethan gripped her arm. "Charlotte," he said. "Something's wrong. I can tell."

She shook her head, jerking away from his touch. "Nothing's wrong. I just need to be . . ." To his surprise, a sob tore from her throat. "Alone."

Before he could stop her, she'd run into the house. For a moment he stood frozen, then dashed in after her. He found her in her bedroom, facedown on the bed. "Charlotte, tell me what's the matter," he insisted, sitting down next to her.

Her face was buried in the pillow, but her shoulders shook with sobs. "Just go away," she said, her voice muffled.

"I'm not going anywhere," said Ethan, placing a hand on the small of her back and rubbing gently, "until you tell me what's going on."

With an abrupt movement, Charlotte sat up. She clasped a pillow to her stomach and looked at him, her face tearstained. He'd never seen her look so scared, so vulnerable, and his heart melted, all fear for himself vanishing in his concern for her.

"I . . . I don't want to tell you." She dropped her eyes. "I don't want to burden you."

"I love you, Charlotte," Ethan reminded her. "Whatever it is, it couldn't be a burden."

She burst into tears again. "I just don't know what to do," she sobbed.

"Is it—is it something to do with your dad?" he guessed. "Your dad and my mom?"

Charlotte shook her tangled blond hair. "Oh, just go home, Ethan," she begged. "And try to forget about me. Take my word for it. You don't want to know. If I tell you, you'll never want to see me again."

"Tell me," Ethan commanded, his voice steady and serious.

Charlotte took a deep, shaky breath. Not meeting his eyes, she stammered, "I—I think I'm—I'm—" She broke down again.

"What?" he pressed, stroking her arm to calm her.

Charlotte lifted her face to his. "Pregnant," she whispered.

Ethan's hand dropped to the bedspread. For a long moment he just stared at her, his face

71

pale with shock. "You're . . . you're . . ."

She jumped up from the bed and started pacing. "I knew I shouldn't have told you," she said, her voice cracking. "It's my problem."

"Wait a minute." Ethan stood up, striding quickly to her side. "It's our problem, Char. We're in it together. After all, it takes two to . . ."

He wanted to ask her a hundred questions. *How do you know? Are you absolutely sure?* And they'd been so careful. Charlotte seemed to read his mind. "Accidents happen." She sniffled. "I'm— I'm so sorry, Ethan." Tears started streaming down her face once more. "I don't want to tangle you up in this. I'll be okay. I'll just defer college for a semester or two. I have the money—I can go someplace and have the baby and put it up for adoption and nobody even needs to know."

The words spilled from her in a torrent. Ethan struggled to grasp the significance of what Charlotte was saying. "Adoption? You mean—"

"I can't do it the other way. I know you're thinking I should get an abortion." Her whole body shuddered as she whispered the word. "That's probably what you think I should do, but I just can't, Ethan. Please don't make me."

"I'm not going to make you do anything," Ethan assured her. He rocked her in his arms, stroking her hair. "Shh. Don't cry. Please, Char. It'll be okay. I promise."

"Just *go*," she begged, her face pressed

against his shoulder. "I can handle it on my own. You can pretend this never happened, you never knew me. It will be better for you that way."

"I'm not going anywhere, Charlotte." Ethan sat down on the edge of the bed, pulling her onto his lap. "Now, listen to me. You don't have to deal with this alone. I'm here for you. I'll always be here for you. If you want to have the baby, I'll—I'll stay with you. Every step of the way."

"Then both our hearts will be broken when it's time to give it up." She buried her face in her hands. "Our baby. Our poor little baby."

Our baby, Ethan repeated to himself. Suddenly he knew what he had to do. There was only one choice, really. Only one right thing. "Char," he said, pulling down her hands and holding them tightly. "Look at me." She gazed at him, blinking away the tears. Her eyes had never appeared so brilliantly blue. "I love you," Ethan told her. "Do you love me?"

Charlotte nodded.

"I'd planned to ask you someday—this is just a little sooner than we expected, that's all. Will you . . ." The magnitude of what he was about to say left him breathless. He cleared his throat and tried again. "Charlotte Ransom, will you marry me?"

Her jaw dropped in astonishment. Ethan stroked her fingers, playing with the silver ring he'd given her the previous summer. "I don't have the money to buy you a diamond," he said, "so this'll have to be our engagement ring for now, but I promise someday . . . I'll take care of you, that's what counts. I won't let you down. So . . . will you, Char?"

Ethan's heart pounded as he waited for Charlotte's answer. The doubts he'd been feeling about the future of their relationship faded, replaced by a rush of hope and love. Hadn't he always dreamed of spending the rest of his life with Charlotte? Of coming back to Silver Beach with her, every summer, forever and ever? *A baby,* he thought, picturing Charlotte with a swaddled infant in her arms. *And she wants to keep it—she doesn't want to give it up. That has to say something about how she feels about me.* There was no doubt about it. A baby would change her, change him, change everything.

"We're going to be parents," Ethan whispered, his eyes shining.

For a long moment Charlotte just stared at him, as if she was measuring the depth of his love and commitment. Then, slowly, she smiled. "Yes, Ethan Wells," she said, clasping her arms around his neck. "I'll marry you."

6

"I typed up Casey's play last night and made copies for everyone. All the characters are vegetables," Elli told her day campers. "Now, who wants to be a potato?"

Five minutes later, all the parts in eight-year-old Casey McAllister's play, *The Magic Garden,* had been divvied up and the children were bolting from the clubhouse to go home for lunch. Elli was flipping through her copy of the script, chuckling, when Sam entered. "I can't wait to see this—Stephen Brewster as Carlton the talking cauliflower," she said. "Where do these kids get their imagination?"

"I don't know, but it's proof that this writing and drama program is important," he replied, slinging an arm around her shoulders. "It gives them a chance to act out all their wackiest ideas."

"How about having lunch at my house?" Elli

suggested as they walked toward the door. "Nana roasted a chicken last night and we have some great leftovers."

"Sounds great, but I only have an hour." He checked his watch. "Make that forty minutes. Driving time," he explained.

Elli squeezed him around the waist. "I know you're busy. Thanks for taking time out to come and see me."

"Are you kidding?" He bent to brush the top of her head with a kiss. "This makes my day."

They'd just reached the door when it swung open. Charlotte sauntered in, wearing a short tennis dress and visor, her long golden hair tied back in a ponytail. "Hey, you two," she sang out. "Have you seen my fiancé?"

Elli laughed. "Your *what?*"

"Fiancé," Charlotte repeated. "Ethan Chapman Wells. Have you seen him?"

Elli looked at Sam, who rolled his eyes. *Typical Charlotte—she has to rub it in my face that she has my brother wrapped around her finger,* Elli thought. "No, I haven't seen him."

"And what's with the fiancé thing?" asked Sam. "You shouldn't joke about stuff like that. That's how rumors get started."

"It just so happens it's not a joke," said Charlotte loftily. "We decided last night."

"Oh, please," said Elli.

"It's true." Charlotte hummed a few bars of

"Here Comes the Bride," smiling. "Aren't you going to congratulate me?"

A queasy feeling percolated in Elli's stomach. *She must be joking—she must be.* "Come on, Char. You're not serious. You can't be."

"I've never been more serious about anything in my life," Charlotte declared. "We're engaged."

Elli paled slightly. "I—I don't believe you," she stuttered.

"You can ask him yourself," said Charlotte, her smile smug. "Why, Eleanor, don't tell me you're not *happy* for us!"

Elli managed to crack a smile. "Yeah, sure. Um, Sam? I'll be right back—I just need to get something at the cottage."

Elli turned on her heel and walked off, trying her best to look nonchalant. *Charlotte's just being Charlotte,* she told herself. *Ethan'll laugh when I tell him.* But as soon as she was out of sight of Sam and Charlotte, she broke into a run.

She found her brother at the house, rummaging through the closet where they stored the sports equipment. "Broke a string," he told his sister, not seeming to notice that she was breathless and wild-eyed, "but I can't find that other good Head racket I brought up here with me."

Elli reached for a tennis ball and tossed it casually in the air, trying to gain control of her breathing. "So, Ethan, you'll never believe what Charlotte's saying about you two."

Ethan straightened. He turned to face her, his eyes shadowed and wary. "What?"

"She's calling you her fiancé." Elli laughed, the sound somewhat forced and shrill. "She just told me and Sam you got engaged last night."

She waited for Ethan to chuckle, to wave a hand in dismissal. Instead, he nodded. "Yeah, we did."

Elli's heart constricted. "You're kidding."

"Nope. It's true."

She felt her knees buckle slightly. "Ethan, are you *insane?*"

"Don't think so," he said with a thin smile.

"You can't be serious." She shook her head in disbelief. "You just can't be serious."

"We're dead serious," Ethan rejoined. "And why shouldn't we be?"

"Because you're only seventeen. You haven't even graduated from high school! I mean, you've only had your driver's license for a year," she added somewhat irrelevantly.

"I'm old enough to know what I want, and so is Charlotte," declared Ethan.

"You're old enough to make total fools of yourselves but you're not old enough to think about getting married," Elli countered.

She drew a few deep breaths, her head starting to clear somewhat. *It's just one of their crazy games,* she told herself, *one of Charlotte's dares. She'll turn it into a way to torture Ethan, and when the novelty wears off, she'll call the whole thing off.* "I just hope you're not going to tell Mom and Dad. I mean, I assume you're planning to wait until you graduate from college, so in that case—"

"We're not waiting," Ethan said quietly.

Elli froze. "What did you say?"

"I said, we're not waiting," Ethan repeated, his voice louder, defiant.

"Why on earth not?" Elli cried. "Ethan, what's going on?"

"Charlotte's pregnant."

Elli took a step backward, sitting down abruptly on the Windsor bench in the hallway. "Pregnant?" she gasped, her face white as paper.

"So we're getting married," Ethan said, as casually as if he were saying, "So we're going out for pizza."

Dazed, Elli put a hand to her forehead. "Getting married. I know this is . . . It's a big deal, and you have to be responsible. But Ethan, you don't have to throw your life away just because—"

"It's not throwing my life away," he broke in angrily. "It's what I want." Reaching into the closet, he grabbed a tennis racket.

"Ethan, listen to me. Marriage isn't the only option. You could—"

"I said it's what I want!" he shouted. "And

nothing you say is going to make me feel differently."

"Ethan, please," Elli begged, stretching out her hand. "Please just—"

But her brother was already gone, the screen door slamming shut behind him. Elli sank back on the bench. *This can't be happening,* she thought. *It's a bad dream. It must be a bad dream.*

That night, the yacht club's Little Club, where the younger Silver Beach residents hung out and partied, was decked with streamers and balloons. People danced wildly to the music blasting from the stereo. A big, hand-printed banner draped over the bar announced the reason for the festivities: *Congratulations, Charlotte and Ethan.*

"This is crazy," Elli muttered to Sam, her jaw clenched. "I can't believe people think this is something to celebrate."

Amber Madden bounced up to them, her arm hooked through Chad Emerson's. "I can't get over your crazy brother," Amber gushed. "This is so romantic! He and Charlotte are going to get married and they don't want to wait more than a month or two! Where will they live? How's he going to finish school?"

"Don't ask me," Elli said grimly.

As Amber and Chad moved on Sam looked across the room at Charlotte, who stood amid a group of excitedly chattering girls. "Do people know the whole story?" Sam asked Elli in a low voice. "I mean, the baby part?"

Elli shrugged. "If they don't, it won't be hard to guess. I mean, why else get married in such a rush?"

"And this happened last night? Just like that?"

"Well, not *just* like that," Elli said dryly. "I guess she told him last night."

"She told him she was pregnant, and he asked her to marry him."

"That's about it."

Sam sipped his beer, the suspicion growing in his heart. *This is a ploy,* he thought. *Charlotte's lying.* He glanced at Elli out of the corner of his eye, started to say something, then bit his tongue. He hadn't told her about the scene a few nights before, when Charlotte had made a pass at him—nothing had come of it, and it would only have upset her to hear how willingly Charlotte would cheat on Ethan. Now he thought again of how mad Charlotte had gotten—she'd seemed to be racing toward some sort of emotional cliff. He could see her doing something reckless and outrageous to get the attention she seemed to need so desperately.

I could ask Charlotte straight out, Sam thought. *Call her bluff. Maybe nip this whole thing in the bud.* "Be right back, Elli," he said. "Can I get you anything at the bar?"

She shook her head. "No, thanks."

Sam made his way through the crowd, his eyes fixed on Charlotte's animated profile. When she saw him coming, her face lit up with triumph. "Hi there, Sammy," she purred, stepping away from the girls.

They stood alone, face to face. Charlotte tilted her head to one side, her lips curved with amusement. "Do you have something to say to me?" she asked.

Sam's mouth went dry. He cleared his throat, struggling to summon the words. *Tell her you know what she's up to,* he commanded himself. *Do it, for Ethan. For Elli.* "I just wanted to say . . ." His voice came out in a croak, and all at once, Sam realized he couldn't. He didn't know for sure Charlotte had lied to Ethan about being pregnant. He had to face it—he didn't know Charlotte. They'd grown up together, and on some levels he felt he understood her, but there would always be a wild, mysterious part of her none of them—not him, and probably not even Ethan—could quite figure out or predict.

"I just wanted to say . . . congratulations," Sam mumbled. He reached out to shake her hand. "Hope you guys'll be happy."

Charlotte laughed. "Oh, we will."

Ethan walked up at that moment and, with a smile at Sam, swept Charlotte onto the dance floor. *Happy,* Sam repeated to himself, watching the couple dance. Was there really any chance of that?

*   *   *

The next morning, Charlotte stood in the front hall at Briarwood and listened to her father arguing with Mrs. Wells, a smug smile on her face. It was easy enough to eavesdrop on the heated conversation taking place in the dining room. Both Mrs. Wells's and Mr. Ransom's voices were raised nearly to shouting level.

"She's your daughter." A coffee cup clattered vehemently onto a saucer. "You could say something to her—you could try for once to control her behavior."

"Her behavior isn't all that's at issue here," Mr. Ransom boomed. "What about your son? Are you saying he's not responsible at all? He's some kind of innocent lamb being led to the slaughter?"

"I didn't say he wasn't responsible," Mrs. Wells protested. "But Charlotte *is* a year older, and from the start she's been a bad influence."

Charlotte bit her lip to keep from laughing out loud. "A bad influence," repeated Mr. Ransom dryly. "It's so easy to label people, isn't it, Grace? You have my daughter conveniently pegged. She's a bad influence, and I suppose that's my fault."

"Well, as a matter of fact . . ."

Charlotte retreated to the kitchen, still smiling. She loved the fuss and attention that the news of her engagement, and the rumor of her pregnancy, had caused. *This is a bonus,* she thought, stirring milk into a mug of hot, strong coffee. *Dad and Mrs. Wells having a major-league spat over me and Ethan.* Maybe they'd break up. Maybe Mrs. Wells wouldn't become her stepmother after all.

Just then Charlotte heard Mrs. Wells stomping down the hallway and out of the house, the front door slamming shut. A few seconds later Mr. Ransom entered the kitchen, breakfast dishes in his hands. At the sight of Charlotte, his scowl deepened. "Morning, Dad," Charlotte drawled.

Mr. Ransom dumped the dishes in the sink. "You're a fool, do you know that? A stupid fool."

Charlotte almost welcomed his harsh words. It was the most attention he'd paid to her in ages. *On some level he must actually care about me,* she thought, with strange hope. "Are you going to forbid me to marry Ethan?" she asked, blowing on her coffee.

"It's your life—I don't give a damn if you marry Ethan," her father said. "But that doesn't mean I don't think you're a fool."

Mr. Ransom left the room and Charlotte swallowed her disappointment along with a mouthful of scalding coffee. The engagement may have caused tears and struggles in the Chapman-Wells household, but not at Briarwood—her father wouldn't stand in her way. *And that's fine with me,* Charlotte decided, a glint of vengeful malice in her eyes. Maybe he didn't give a damn what Charlotte did with her life, but he gave a damn about Grace Wells. And Charlotte had a pleasant suspicion that the morning's altercation between her father and his lover was just the beginning.

Mrs. Wells swept into the breakfast room just as Elli, Ethan, and their grandmother were sitting down with bowls of cereal and cups of coffee. Without preamble, she burst into angry speech. "I won't have it."

Ethan cocked one eyebrow. "Won't have what, Mom?"

Elli held her breath. Ethan's tone was like gasoline on a fire; their mother's face flamed a furious red. "Don't you dare be fresh on top of everything else," Mrs. Wells snapped. "You're still a member of this family, and I expect you to behave with some courtesy."

Ethan held his ground. "I just asked a question."

"You know damn well what I'm talking about," his mother rejoined. "This ridiculous stunt—getting engaged."

"It's not a stunt," Ethan declared.

Elli tightened her grip on her coffee mug.

"Oh, yes it is," said Mrs. Wells. "If you think for one second that I'll let you go through with it, then you're—"

"It's not a question of your letting me do

anything," Ethan broke in. "I can make my own decisions."

"Not this one. You're only seventeen—you haven't even finished high school! No, Ethan Chapman Wells, as long as you're living under my roof—"

"If that's the choice you're going to give me . . ." Ethan shoved his chair back and rose to his feet. "I won't live under your roof, Mom."

Mrs. Wells folded her arms across her chest. "And where will you go? How do you suppose you'll take care of yourself, much less a wife and—and—"

"I'll manage." Ethan crossed the kitchen, then turned. "But thanks for understanding, Mom. Thanks for supporting me in this."

They heard his feet pound up the stairs. A door slammed. All at once, Mrs. Wells's shoulders crumpled. "What am I going to do?" she sobbed, burying her face in her hands. "I can't let him—but how can I—" Turning, she too darted from the room.

Elli looked down at her bowl of soggy cereal, then across the table at her grandmother. "Better than a soap opera, huh?" she said with a weak smile.

Mrs. Chapman took a sip of coffee. "I don't know why, but I'm not surprised. Somehow the whole situation just seems so . . . so *Charlotte*."

"It does, doesn't it?" Elli frowned. "She's

always had Ethan under her thumb, manipulating him, pulling his strings like a puppet. Remember when they were kids, how she used to dare him to do all those crazy, stupid things, like walk on the yacht club roof in a thunderstorm? This is the biggest dare yet, only it's about the rest of his life."

"At the same time, the girl is pregnant," Mrs. Chapman pointed out. "They both had something to do with that." She smiled wryly. "It's funny, actually. We're all acting so shocked and outraged and panicked, but really, it's the oldest story in the world."

The oldest story in the world, Elli mused a short while later as she rinsed the breakfast dishes and placed them in the dishwasher. Maybe so, but this was Ethan and Charlotte they were talking about, not two random strangers. Tears pricked Elli's eyelids. *What's going to happen to my brother?*

"Would you look at that," Charlotte said playfully a few mornings later, observing Elli and Sam at work on the *Morning Mist.* "It's actually starting to look like a boat again. Like it might even *float.*"

At the sound of Charlotte's voice, Elli's spine stiffened. She clenched her teeth.

Sam glanced at Elli. "Yep, she's almost seaworthy," he responded with false heartiness.

"Another weekend of work, and we'll be out on the lake in her."

"What a labor of love. It's just too romantic," said Charlotte snidely. "You'll have to let me and Ethan take her for a sail. Would you? To celebrate our engagement?"

She was looking straight at Elli, who couldn't avoid her gaze any longer. "Sure," said Elli tightly.

Charlotte stepped closer to Elli, lowering her voice so that Sam couldn't hear. "Try to show a little more enthusiasm, Eleanor," she purred. "After all, we're going to be sisters. We're going to be sharing everything."

Elli choked back an angry retort, her hands balling into fists. *I don't want to share anything with you,* she wanted to cry. *Especially Ethan!*

Charlotte's attention shifted again. "Ethan!" Ethan strode across the grass to join them on the beach. "Did you take your stuff over to Briarwood?" she asked, hooking her arm possessively through his.

Ethan nodded. Elli tipped her head to one side. "What do you mean?" she asked her brother.

"Mr. Ransom just left on a book-signing trip," he explained, "so I'm moving in with Char. I've got to get out of the house until Mom cools off."

Elli frowned. "And you don't think that's just going to make her madder?"

Ethan turned away from his sister to gaze deep into Charlotte's eyes. "It's what we want to do," he said.

"C'mon, Ethan." Charlotte flashed a triumphant smile at Elli, then tugged on Ethan's hand. "Let's go up to the cottage. I'll help you unpack."

As the two strolled off Elli stood motionless by the boat, her arms hanging at her sides and a dull expression in her eyes. "Earth to Elli," Sam said gently after several moments. "Grab that can of varnish and get a move on."

Elli sighed. "I just . . . can't."

"We could be finished this weekend," Sam urged. "Midsummer Madness weekend. And the weather's been perfect. Aren't you dying to sail this boat? *Our* boat?"

Elli put her hand on her temple. "It just doesn't matter to me anymore," she confessed. "I'm sorry."

Sam rubbed her back tenderly. "I know you're upset, but it's not the end of the world. Not for Ethan, and not for us."

"But it *is* the end of the world for Ethan!" Elli cried. "Getting married and becoming a parent while he's still in high school—do you really think that's the recipe for a good future? I mean, it's not like marriage is easy under the best of circumstances. If it were, so many people wouldn't get divorced." She turned away, not

89

wanting Sam to see the tears coursing down her face. "I'm going to take a swim. I'll see you later."

Tearing off the loose T-shirt she wore over her one-piece bathing suit, Elli jogged toward the water's edge. She waded into the cove, diving as soon as the water hit her waist.

With strong, steady strokes, she swam toward Blueberry Island. *Think about the swim race this weekend,* she commanded herself. *Think about your strategy for winning it.* But she couldn't. She couldn't tear her mind away from Ethan. Ethan, who seemed so helpless as his destiny shrank around him. Ethan, diving into water much deeper and heavier than this. Elli swam faster, harder, but she felt weak and useless. Because her brother was drowning, and she could do nothing to save him.

Charlotte woke on Friday morning with a familiar feeling of dread curdling in her stomach. For a moment she lay on her side, her back to Ethan, and stared out the window, her whole body tense. *Midsummer Madness*, she thought, the memories stirring inside her like a witch's poisonous brew.

Ever since she was eight years old, the anniversary of her mother's death on Midsummer Madness weekend had held horrors for Charlotte. She'd relived the event each year: finding her mother's lifeless body facedown in the shallow waters of the cove; running for her father, then seeing him in the Chapmans' driveway with Elli and Mrs. Wells, laughing as he taught Elli how to ride her new ten-speed bicycle. Each year the fear and sorrow she'd buried surged closer and closer to the surface, goading Charlotte to find

91

solace and forgetfulness any way she could.

Two summers ago, I finally got Dad to admit it had been suicide, Charlotte remembered, turning her pillow so the pillowcase would be cool under her cheek. *And last summer . . .*

Last summer, she'd found the letters. Or rather, Elli had found the letters, hidden in the Chapman cottage attic. Love letters from Holling Ransom to Grace Wells, from a married man to the married woman who lived next door to him at Silver Beach. Love letters written a decade before, early in the season of the very same summer that Mrs. Ransom drowned herself.

Charlotte rolled onto her back, and then over to her other side. She draped an arm and a leg across Ethan's sleeping form. Gradually the tension drained from her limbs and a smile spread across her face. This Midsummer Madness felt different. It *was* different. She wasn't any longer a victim, raging about what other people had done to her, taken from her. Charlotte's arms tightened around Ethan. Finally she was getting her revenge—she was taking something back.

"Breakfast is ready," Ethan called out to Charlotte, who was standing on the deck in her bathrobe drinking a cup of coffee.

Charlotte stepped through the sliding glass door and sat down at the table. Ethan deposited a heaping plate in front of her. "An omelette, whole-wheat toast, fresh fruit," he announced, "and I'm going to squeeze you some juice. Dig in."

Charlotte wrinkled her nose at the food, then pushed the plate away.

Ethan frowned. "You need to eat," he told her. "Good nutrition is really important for the baby."

"But I'm not hungry."

"Oh—right." Ethan rubbed Charlotte's shoulder sympathetically. "Morning sickness?"

"I guess." She shrugged. "I'll just have another cup of coffee."

"I don't know about drinking so much coffee," Ethan said, looking at her with concern. "Isn't caffeine bad for you?"

"I don't really give a damn," Charlotte said impatiently. "Jeez, Ethan. When did you become Dr. Spock?"

He sat down next to her, his expression sheepish. "Sorry. I just care about you, Char. I want you to stay healthy."

"Don't I look healthy?" she asked with a teasing smile.

"You look . . ." He bent forward to brush her lips with a kiss. ". . . spectacularly beautiful."

"So don't worry so much." She held out her coffee cup. "I'll eat a big, disgustingly nutritious lunch. Promise."

Charlotte finished her coffee while Ethan ate the eggs he'd made for her. When she went upstairs to shower, he washed the dishes, then wiped the kitchen counter clean of crumbs. *This isn't so hard,* he thought to himself as he switched off the automatic coffeemaker, emptying the pot into his own cup. *If we take it just one day at a time.*

Ten minutes later, Charlotte breezed downstairs, looking bright and fresh in crisp tennis whites. "I just need to put on my sneakers," Ethan said.

"They're under the bed," she told him. "I'll wait for you on the porch."

He dashed upstairs, put on his sneakers, then came back down again. As he walked toward the screen door he heard Charlotte's voice. She was on the porch, talking to someone on the lawn below her. "Morning, Mrs. Wells," Charlotte called out cheerily. "Or should I start calling you Mom?"

"If you really think," said Mrs. Wells, her tone clipped and harsh, "that you'll ever be my daughter-in-law . . ."

Ethan hurried out the door to Charlotte's side. "Watch it, Mom," he said, putting a protective arm around Charlotte's waist.

"It's you I want to talk to, Ethan," said Mrs. Wells. "Alone. Now."

"We're busy," Ethan replied. "We have to teach the tennis clinic. Maybe some other—"

"Now. Please," his mother added in a more placating tone.

Ethan looked at Charlotte. She shrugged carelessly. "See you on the courts," she said.

Ethan remained standing on the porch, looking down. "What is it, Mom?"

"I'd like you . . . I'd like you to come home. I think we'd have a better chance of straightening this out if you were home with your family instead of here with—with—"

"With my fiancée." Ethan emphasized the word. "I'm staying here. You gave me a choice the other night, remember? You told me to break off with Charlotte or get out of your house."

Mrs. Wells shook her head, her eyes wide with distress. "I didn't mean for it to sound like an ultimatum, for any of this to feel final. Let's not rush into anything. Please, Ethan. There must be some common ground. Can't we talk?"

"Not if your agenda is still to talk me out of marrying Charlotte," Ethan said firmly. "Forget it. Save your breath."

Mrs. Wells opened her mouth, then snapped it shut again. For a long moment she just stared at her son, her brow furrowed with distress. Then she turned away to hurry back across the lawn.

Ethan's heart was thundering in his chest. Why was he so shaken up, now that she had left him alone? Why did he suddenly feel so helpless? *You're right,* he suddenly wanted to confess. *I am too young. I don't know what in hell I'm doing. Help me. Get me out of this.*

He straightened his shoulders, shoving the cowardly thoughts under the surface. He wasn't a little boy anymore, a weakling who needed his mother. He'd chosen his path. He was committed.

"That was pretty good," Sam said, looking down at the stopwatch as Elli waded from the cove late Friday afternoon. "Not your best time, but pretty good."

Elli grabbed a beach towel and began blotting the water from her body. "Fast enough to win?" she asked, even though at this point she didn't much care about the annual swim race to Blueberry Island.

"Maybe." He took the towel from her hands and used it to massage her shoulders. "How about a hot shower and a rubdown?" He tickled her waist. "Back at my house?"

She looked distractedly into the distance. "I need to get back," she said. "I need to head home and— Well, I've been out all day."

Sam gripped her arms, forcing her to look at him. "Elli," he said sternly, "I know you're bummed about Ethan and Charlotte. But there's no point wasting your energy worrying about them. You've got to focus. On the race, on the boat—on us."

Elli shook her head. "I just can't think about anything else," she whispered apologetically. "And I can't stand off to the side while Ethan flushes his life down the toilet. I'm sorry, but I can't."

Sam dropped his hands from her arms. "I wish I could help you help him. But he doesn't want to be helped."

"That doesn't mean I shouldn't try." Elli wrapped the damp towel around her waist. "See you later, okay?"

Not even waiting for Sam's reply, she hurried across the sand and then cut across the yacht club lawn. *Should I shower first?* she wondered as she set a course for Briarwood. If she was warm and dry, maybe she'd feel stronger, and she knew she needed all the strength she could get. Because it wasn't Ethan she planned to confront this time. It was Charlotte.

But she was feeling too desperate to waste a minute on a shower. Climbing the porch steps, she knocked on the front door of the Ransoms' cottage. "Anybody home?" she called through the screen.

Charlotte appeared in the hallway. "Look what the cat dragged in," she said, raising an eyebrow at Elli's wet, disheveled hair and dripping bathing suit.

Elli rubbed her upper arms, which were starting to get goose bumps. "Charlotte, I need to talk to you."

Charlotte stepped out on the porch and stood facing Elli, her expression cool and superior. "What about?"

"You know," said Elli. "About your . . . engagement."

"Don't tell me." Charlotte's mouth curved in a wicked smile. "You want to be my maid of honor."

"Char, it isn't a joke," Elli burst out. "This is serious. We're talking about Ethan's life. His future."

"And my life," said Charlotte, her lips tightening. "My future."

"But he's so young," Elli said, ignoring Charlotte's last statement. "He has so much to look forward to. He really doesn't know what he's doing. Don't make him go through with it."

Charlotte tossed her head scornfully. "I'm not *making* him do anything. Getting married was his idea. He asked me, not the other way around."

"Because he felt he had to," Elli argued. "He felt like he didn't have any other choice. But you *do* have choices, both of you. And if you released Ethan from his promise, you could—"

"It's not going to happen," Charlotte informed Elli bluntly. "You know why? Because I don't want to release him, and what's more, he doesn't want to *be* released. This may be your worst nightmare, Elli, but it's Ethan's dream—having me forever and ever."

"It's a mistake," Elli whispered, "for both of you. Please, Char. Please reconsider."

Charlotte lifted her chin. "Never in a million

years," she declared with a triumphant laugh. "He belongs to me now, not to you. And that's the way it's going to stay."

Turning on her heel, Charlotte sailed back into the house, leaving Elli alone on the shadowy porch. Somewhere inside the house a door slammed, and to Elli it sounded like a prison door. Ethan was trapped inside, tangled in Charlotte's sticky web, and he would never, ever get free.

At sunset, as Elli was picking vegetables in the garden, a black Lexus pulled into the gravel driveway of the Chapman cottage. As the driver stepped out she hurried to greet him. "Dad!" she cried in surprise. "What are you doing here?"

Arthur Wells brushed his daughter's cheek with a distracted kiss. "Your mother called me," he explained. "I'm here to try to talk some sense into your brother."

"Good luck," Elli muttered.

"This is really serious, huh?" said Mr. Wells.

"Yeah."

They walked together toward the house. At the sound of the car, Mrs. Wells had appeared on the porch. "Hello, Arthur," she called.

Mr. Wells climbed the steps to stand next to his ex-wife. "Hello, Grace," he replied, touching her arm briefly.

Elli watched them, openly curious. It had been so long since she'd seen them side by side, or even in the same room. *They look good together,* she thought with a nostalgic pang. *Why couldn't it have worked out for them?*

Mr. Wells sat down in one of the old rocking chairs. "So, tell me more about what's going on."

Mrs. Wells clasped her hands together, rubbing her knuckles. "When I told him he couldn't go through with this, that if he wanted to live under my roof he had to at least back up a few steps and hear me out, he just moved over to Charlotte's."

"And Holling doesn't have a problem with that?" Mr. Wells raised his eyebrows.

"He's out of town. I phoned him, too. Oh, it's all my fault." Mrs. Wells's voice cracked, and she lifted a hand to her eyes. "I let Ethan run wild—I wasn't there for him, didn't set a stable, responsible example." Elli saw a tear trickle down her mother's cheek. "And now I can't even talk to my own son."

Mr. Wells rose to his feet to put a comforting arm around her shoulders. "We did our best," he said quietly.

Elli had to strain to hear her mother's voice, which had dropped to a whisper. "I just can't stand to see him make such a big mistake. I don't want him to regret this for the rest of his life. I want my children to be happy."

For a long moment Mr. Wells studied his ex-wife's downcast face. Then he asked, "Where is he? Next door?"

Mrs. Wells nodded.

Elli trailed her father into the house. She heard him on the kitchen phone. "Ethan, this is your dad. No, I'm here at the cottage and I'd like to talk to you. Now, please."

At the sound of her father's brisk, self-assured, caring tone, Elli's hopes soared, but only for a moment. She knew Ethan respected their father more than anyone. But at this point, was there a person on earth who could change Ethan's mind?

Ethan walked slowly across the lawn between Briarwood and his family's cottage, feeling like a little kid about to be spanked. He could see his father, sitting alone on the porch in the twilight.

The best defense is a good offense, Ethan told himself as he mounted the steps. "I can't believe you drove all this way to talk to me, Dad," he said casually. "Why didn't you just call?"

"Because your mother was practically having a nervous breakdown," Mr. Wells replied sternly. "I've never heard her so upset."

"I don't see why she should be upset," said Ethan, sticking his hands in his trouser pockets. "This isn't her crisis. This is about me and Charlotte, and we're handling it."

"You're too young to get married, son. That's the bottom line."

"The bottom line is, Charlotte's pregnant,"

Ethan countered flatly, "and she doesn't like the idea of having an abortion and I'd never push her to do something she didn't want to do."

"What about adoption?"

Ethan stared at his father. "You really think I would let her go through pregnancy and labor and all that and then just hand her baby—our baby—over to some stranger?"

Mr. Wells gripped the arms of the rocking chair. "You can't just think about now, about what would hurt now. You have to think about the future. What about college? A career? Are you really ready to start raising a family, Ethan, before you've even earned a high-school diploma?"

Ethan slapped the porch railing with his hand. "Did I say I thought it would be easy? We know what we're up against. But we love each other. We're not going to screw this up, Dad. Not like you and Mom screwed up."

Ethan saw his father's face pale, and a surge of satisfaction rushed through his veins. *Well, someone had to say it,* he thought exultantly. *Someone had to speak the truth.* Before Mr. Wells could respond, Ethan jogged back down the steps and disappeared into the night.

"A movie? Thanks, but I'm not really in the mood," Elli told Sam over the phone. "I think I'll just go to bed early, so I'll be fresh for the race tomorrow."

"You know best," Sam replied. "I love you."

"I love you, too. Bye."

She replaced the receiver and looked out the window of her bedroom. The wind had picked up, and tree branches tossed wildly against the star-speckled sky. *Midsummer Madness is here again,* thought Elli, opening her window so the breeze could ripple the curtains. *And everyone's going crazy, just like they always do this time of year.*

She hadn't told Sam the whole truth. She *should* go to bed early in order to be well rested for the next day's swim race, but she was far from feeling sleepy. The situation with Ethan, and her father's presence in one of the second-floor guest rooms, had raised the tension level in the house to a fever pitch. *None of us will sleep a wink tonight,* Elli predicted silently.

Deciding a walk on the beach was her best shot at clearing her mind, she padded across the room and then into the hall and down the stairs. Outside, the grass was dewy under her bare feet, the sand cool. She walked north up the beach at the very edge of the water, splashing as she went.

She turned around before she reached Eagle Cottage. She didn't want to run into Sam, and not only because she'd told him she was going right to sleep. Ordinarily, she'd love to share an exhilarating, windy night like this with Sam, but lately she'd been holding back a little, clinging to her privacy. *Because he doesn't understand about Ethan, about how I have to take care of him,* she realized. *He's never really understood.*

Too soon, she was back on the beach in front of her own cottage. Not ready to go back inside, Elli sat down in the shelter of a grassy dune. She hugged her knees, her eyes on the dark lake, listening to the rhythmic lap of the waves.

She was starting to relax when she heard the voices of two people walking along the sand. They stopped just a stone's throw away, oblivious to Elli, who was hidden by the shadow of the dune.

"You said it was an emergency, Grace, so I cut short my book tour," the man said. Elli immediately recognized the voice, the chiseled profile: Mr. Ransom. "But exactly what do you expect me to do?"

"Be a father to Charlotte," Mrs. Wells answered. "Reason with her. Stop this ridiculous marriage from taking place."

"Is that what you think fathers do?" asked Mr. Ransom. "Prohibit? Forbid? Do you really think a lecture is going to solve the problem here?"

"But you don't even try!" cried Mrs. Wells. "You're shirking your responsibility, Holling—you have been for years. Children need guidance, rules, limits."

"Charlotte's not a child. She's eighteen," Mr. Ransom pointed out coldly, "and I'll thank you not to tell me how to be a parent to her."

Elli shifted uncomfortably on the sand, hunching her shoulders to make herself smaller. With an effort, she resisted the temptation to crawl off through the dune grass. She didn't want to have to listen to this argument, but she knew if she made the slightest move, her mother and Mr. Ransom would hear and they'd all be incredibly embarrassed. And she *was* curious despite herself. She'd just have to stay put until they left.

And they showed no signs of leaving. "Just this once," Mrs. Wells begged Mr. Ransom, her voice pitched high with emotion. "I'm only asking you to step in this once. Tell her no, Holling. It's what's best for her—what's best for my son."

"Interfering like that goes against all my principles," he declared firmly. Then his tone modulated, softened. "Grace, listen to yourself. 'Step in, say no.' Do you really think they'll respond to that approach? If they're this much in love—"

"They're too young to be in love."

"No younger than we were when *we* fell in love," Mr. Ransom rejoined. "I was eighteen and you were seventeen—exactly the same ages as Charlotte and Ethan."

Elli's jaw dropped open in astonishment. *Eighteen and seventeen—the same ages as Charlotte and Ethan?*

"We were different," she heard her mother murmur in protest. "They're just children."

105

"You think of them as children because they're *our* children," Mr. Ransom argued. "They consider themselves adults, just the way you and I did. And what if we'd been as brave as they are? What if we'd followed our hearts instead of our heads?"

Elli's mind was spinning. *I'm not hearing right,* she thought, confused. *They had an affair ten years ago—they were in their thirties, not their teens.*

"It wouldn't have worked—that's what everyone told us," said Mrs. Wells. "We were in love, but it was so crazy and unpredictable. My parents sent me away to school."

"Yes. We went our separate ways, married other people. But it was no use, Grace." Mr. Ransom put his hand on her waist. "Do you remember? Do you remember how hard we struggled to keep our feelings buried?"

Mrs. Wells hid her face in her hands. "Not hard enough. Arthur and I were still practically newlyweds, and we came here for our summer vacation . . ."

"And I had Annette, but it didn't matter," Mr. Ransom said hoarsely. "You were the only one I'd ever wanted."

"I was so weak," sobbed Mrs. Wells. "Why didn't I have the strength to take Arthur and leave Silver Beach, leave you? Before—before—"

"It wouldn't have done any good. Sooner or

later, we would have found our way back to each other. And do you really regret that summer?" Mr. Ransom's voice dropped to a passionate whisper. "That beautiful summer?"

Mrs. Wells shook her head. Stepping closer, she leaned against him. "No. I can't regret that summer—I can't regret our love. It would mean wishing Elli had never been born."

The words of her last sentence writhed through the night air like a cold snake, and Elli shuddered. *No,* she thought wildly. *It can't be.*

Mr. Ransom wrapped an arm around Mrs. Wells. "Love isn't ever wrong, Grace," he said quietly. "It's the only thing we can trust. The only thing we can believe in."

Gradually their voices faded as they continued down the beach. Elli sprang to her feet, her heart thundering in her chest. She stared after the middle-aged couple walking away in the moonlight, and slowly she felt the truth penetrating her like the blade of a sword. "Arthur and I were still practically newlyweds . . . That beautiful summer . . . It would mean wishing Elli had never been born . . ."

Mom and Mr. Ransom . . . my parents.

8

Elli tossed and turned all night long. Whenever she woke, her discovery was seared into her mind in large letters, as if with a flaming-hot brand. *Holling Ransom is my father.*

She rose with the first faint light of dawn and began pacing her bedroom. "I can't believe it," she whispered, gazing out the window at the mist on the lake. "Maybe I was dreaming. I didn't actually walk on the beach, didn't see them and hear them."

But she knew this was wishful thinking. She recalled every single word of her mother's conversation with Mr. Ransom—she could hear it playing over and over, like a tape. *It didn't start ten years ago, right before Mrs. Ransom died,* Elli thought. *Mom was in love with him when she was my age.* Suddenly Elli remembered a discovery she'd made two summers before, when she and Sam won the Midsummer Madness sailing regatta. Holding the silver cup that came with victory, she'd been surprised to see her mother's and Mr. Ransom's names engraved on the cup along with those of all the winners for the whole long history of the race. Her mother and Mr. Ransom had won the regatta when they were teenagers, sailing Mr. Ransom's yacht *Dandelion*. "I didn't know you sailed when you were young, Mom," Elli had said, "and you were pretty good!" Mrs. Wells had just shrugged. "I guess I outgrew it," she'd answered.

She outgrew her love of sailing, but she didn't outgrow her love for Mr. Ransom, thought Elli. *They broke up, but then they got back together—after they were married to other people. And then . . . and then . . .*

She put her hands to her face, lightly touching her cheekbones, her chin, her nose, her forehead. As she explored her features she felt strangely disembodied. *I'm not who I think I am. Dad's not my dad, he's just Mom's husband, or rather ex-husband. And Ethan's only my half brother. Holling Ransom is my real father. Which means Charlotte . . . Charlotte . . .*

Crossing the room, Elli stood in front of the mirror over the dresser and stared at her reflection. Ethan and her mother both had green eyes; her father—or Mr. Wells, the man she'd always thought was her father—had hazel ones. How could she not have wondered about her own clear blue eyes? Mr. Ransom's eyes. Charlotte's eyes. *Charlotte—my half sister.*

A shudder racked Elli's body and she stumbled backward, collapsing on the edge of the bed. *He's my father and she's my sister.* And Mr. Ransom knew it. *That's why he was always so nice to me,* Elli realized. *Nicer to me than he was to Charlotte.* But did Mr. Wells know he *wasn't* Elli's father?

Suddenly Elli knew she had to get out of the house or she'd explode. Flinging off her nightgown, she slipped into a swimsuit, shorts, and a T-shirt. She ran quietly downstairs, then nearly collided with someone coming out of the kitchen. "Dad!" Elli squeaked. "You're up early!"

"I brought some work with me," Mr. Wells explained. "I was just making some coffee and toast. Want some?"

Elli found herself gaping at him. Hazel eyes, sandy hair turning gray, a slightly receding chin. *I don't look anything like you,* she wanted to shout. *Didn't you ever notice that? This whole family is built on a lie—don't you know that?*

"N-no, thanks. This morning I'm in the swim race," Elli stammered. "Can't eat—gotta run—"

She flew out the front door before Mr. Wells could respond. Sprinting straight to the lake, she plunged in, not caring that her T-shirt and shorts were getting soaked.

She submerged herself in the lake, but it

didn't help. Her thoughts continued to tumble and wheel like swooping gulls scattered by a storm. How could she ever feel like her feet were on solid ground again? Elli wasn't who she thought she was. No one was.

Elli adjusted her swim goggles, then bent her knees slightly and leaned forward at the waist, tensing herself in preparation to dive. Right before walking down the dock, she'd spotted Ethan and Charlotte—her half sister—and nearly freaked out at the sight. *I'm jumping out of my skin,* Elli thought. *If the starting gun doesn't go off soon . . .*

Crack. The gun sounded and she dove off the dock, her body slicing into the water of the cove. On all sides of her, other swimmers also struck out for Blueberry Island, but she didn't pay any attention to them. She focused only on her own strokes, her arms lifting and pulling, her legs kicking. Adrenaline coursed through her veins and she knew she was swimming faster than she'd ever swum in her life.

The sound of cheering voices confirmed her feeling. As she waded into the shallows, racing to be the first to reach the beach, she realized she *was* the first. She'd won.

The cluster of spectators who'd been waiting on the island for the competing swimmers burst into applause. Sam hurried forward, a towel in his hands and a broad grin on his face. "You did it, Wells!" he shouted, wrapping the towel and his arms around her body.

Elli managed the weakest of smiles. Dick Courtland handed her the prize, a gold medal on a green and white ribbon. She took it without speaking, then walked away from the crowd.

Sam hurried after her. "Are you okay, El? You're still shivering like crazy." He rubbed her arms and shoulders vigorously with the towel. "Maybe you're just excited. You won the race!"

Elli shook her head, hiding her eyes behind a tangle of wet hair. Pushing Sam away, she continued to walk down the beach. In a few long strides he caught up to her again, stopping her with a hand on her arm. "Hold on, Elli," he commanded. "What's wrong?"

Elli hadn't planned to tell him—not there, not then—but she felt the words bubbling up in her chest like the hot steam of a geyser. "It's . . . it's . . . oh, God, Sam. My mom—last night, on the beach with Mr. Ransom." She looked into Sam's bemused, expectant face, her eyes wide with distress. "I heard them talking. About the past—the long-ago past. Before I was born. When they were young and—and— Sam, Mr. Ransom is . . . he's . . ."

She choked on the words. Sam stared at her, a strange expression flickering across his face. "He's what?" he pressed, gripping her arms tighter.

Elli licked her lips, which suddenly were as

dry as paper. "He's my father," she whispered.

Sam drew in his breath sharply.

"I know. It's crazy—it's unbelievable," Elli went on. "It turns out they've been in love *forever*. They grew up together—it's like me and you, or Ethan and Charlotte. I guess they broke up when they were young but then they started an affair after Mom married Dad, after Mr. Ransom married Annette, and it must have been going on all those years, up until the time Mrs. Ransom killed herself. And—"

Elli realized she was babbling. She also realized that, after that first intake of breath, Sam was listening to her almost calmly. Where was the shock, the outrage, the disbelief? "Sam?" she said, her voice rising on a questioning note.

He shook his head, as if his thoughts had drifted for a moment and he needed to bring himself back to her, back to the moment. "Wow, Elli," he mumbled. "No wonder you're freaked out. This is wild."

"It's like a nightmare." Elli's teeth started chattering. "God, Sam. I just don't know if I can deal with it."

"Look at you—your lips are turning blue." He bundled her in the towel, folding her in his arms. "I know it seems like the end of the world, but it'll be okay, Elli. I promise."

She rested her head against his chest, trying to focus on the measured beating of his heart. It felt good to unburden herself to him. She wanted to believe him, wanted to believe that everything would be okay.

"But it *is* the end of the world, in a way," Elli said, her voice low and strained. "I just wish we could stay here on the island forever. I don't want to go back to Silver Beach, Sam. Not ever."

"The theme for the costume ball tonight is the sixties," said Mrs. Wells, looking up from the clothes she was sorting through as Elli entered the living room at noon. "Just look at this stuff." She held up a pair of garish striped bell-bottoms and laughed. "Love beads, peace signs, patches, fringe. And of course *everything's* one hundred percent polyester."

Elli took a deep breath. She knew she had to spit out the words now, while they were alone in the house and before she lost her nerve. "Mom, I know the truth," she announced.

Mrs. Wells tilted her head to one side.

"I know," Elli repeated, balling her hands into fists. "About you and Mr. Ransom."

Her mother looked at her through guarded eyes. "The truth about what?" Mrs. Wells said carefully.

"About your affair. When it really started." Elli kept her eyes glued to her mother's face. "I heard you talking last night. On the beach."

Mrs. Wells wrinkled her forehead in a puzzled

frown. Then slowly the color drained from her face. "You heard us," she whispered, "when we were talking about . . ."

"About me," Elli confirmed, her voice shaky. "About him being my . . . my father."

Mother and daughter stared at each other. Elli waited, hoping against hope that her mother would deny the allegation. *Tell me it didn't really happen that way,* Elli prayed. *You didn't cheat on Dad. You didn't have another man's baby, and that baby isn't me.*

Mrs. Wells sank weakly back against the sofa cushions, still clutching the bell-bottom pants. Elli's hopes died. "I didn't ever want you to find out," Mrs. Wells said. "I didn't want anyone to find out."

"You mean Dad doesn't know?" asked Elli. "He doesn't know he's not my . . . I'm not his daughter?" Her face crumpled, and a tear rolled down her cheek.

"You *are* his daughter," Mrs. Wells declared passionately. "He raised you. He loves you."

"But maybe he wouldn't if he knew," Elli choked out. "God, Mom, how could you? How could you do that to him? How could you do that to *me?*"

Mrs. Wells buried her face in her hands, and her shoulders shook with suppressed sobs. "If you knew how much pain it's caused me . . ."

Elli didn't care about her mother's pain.

"Don't try to make me feel sorry for you, Mom," she said, her voice trembling. "It won't work. You're not the victim here."

"I don't want you to feel sorry for me. I just want you to try to understand how—"

"I'll never understand," Elli broke in. "I don't *want* to understand." She backed away from her mother, her wild eyes glistening with tears. "I just want to forget what I heard, erase it from my mind. I want to, but I'll never be able to. Never."

She turned away. "Elli, wait," her mother called in a desperate voice. "Where are you going? Promise you won't tell anyone—you won't tell Arthur, or Ethan."

"No," said Elli as she bolted for the door. "I won't promise. I don't owe you silence, Mom. I don't owe you loyalty. I don't owe you anything."

Late in the afternoon, Elli joined Sam by the boat shed to put the finishing touches on the rebuilt *Morning Mist.* "Isn't she beautiful?" asked Sam, stepping back to admire the trim, graceful sailboat. "I can't wait to get her out on the lake, see how she handles. I bet we'll be ready tomorrow."

Elli eyed the boat without much interest. The project that had engrossed them for the entire summer no longer had much meaning for her. "Hmm," she mumbled, picking up a paintbrush.

"I know you're upset," Sam said quietly. "But what you found out—it doesn't really change anything. Your parents are still your parents, and you're still you."

Elli lost what slender hold she had on her nerves. "You're so far from understanding how I feel, it's almost funny," she snapped. "It changes *everything*. My relationships with absolutely everyone. And the worst part is . . ." The nauseous feeling percolated in her stomach. "Charlotte Ransom is my *sister*."

"Your half sister," Sam corrected her, "but she doesn't know, and doesn't ever need to know."

"But *I* know. And what does it say about me? If Charlotte is my half sister, if we share a father, the same blood . . . then I must be like her in some ways."

"You're nothing like her," Sam assured Elli. "Apples and oranges. It just goes to show that blood doesn't always count for that much."

Elli wasn't convinced. She felt something stir deep inside her, something elemental and instinctive. *We always hated each other, me and Charlotte. But something always held us together, closer than either of us liked.*

Suddenly Elli felt claustrophobic and trapped. Trapped by Silver Beach, by her blood, by her fate. "I don't want Charlotte as a sister. By blood *or* by marriage." A new wave of anxiety and distaste washed over her. "Sam, I didn't even think about how this affects Ethan!"

Sam raised his eyebrows quizzically. "How does it affect Ethan?"

"Don't you see? It makes it even worse, him marrying Charlotte," said Elli. "If I'm his sister and she's my half sister, then it's almost like . . . like incest."

"I think you're overreacting," said Sam.

Elli shook her head. "I have to get Ethan away from here. We *both* have to get away. This sick connection between our family and the Ransoms . . . it has to end. The marriage has to be stopped."

Sam rested his hand on the sailboat. "There's not much chance of stopping it at this point, is there? I mean, even if you told Ethan that Mr. Ransom is your real father, that Char's your half sister. She's not related to him—it's not incest. Everyone's tried to talk them out of getting married, but as far as I can tell, it's only made them more committed to the idea. Maybe it's time to stand back and let them do it."

"No," said Elli stubbornly.

"We've had this conversation before," said Sam, an edge of frustration in his voice. "You don't really have a choice, Elli. Let Ethan live his own life, make his own mistakes."

Elli's anger flared. "I won't let him make *this* mistake—it's too serious. He's my brother and I love him. Don't you understand loyalty?"

Sam looked almost impatient. "Sure, I

understand loyalty. But I also know hysteria when I see it."

Elli flinched. "Hysteria?"

"That came out wrong," he said quickly. "But Elli, I really think you're overreacting."

He reached out for her, but she took a step away. Suddenly she saw something with perfect clarity. "I'm not overreacting," she said, "you're *under*reacting. This whole mess my family's in—you act like it's no big deal, like it's old news."

Sam's eyes shifted away from hers. "Well, maybe not old news, but . . ."

"But what?" she pressed. She thought about their conversation on Blueberry Island that morning. *He didn't even really react then,* she recalled. "What's going on, Sam? Don't tell me you—" A terrible, almost impossible thought occurred to her. "Don't tell me you already *knew.*"

Sam didn't answer right away. He didn't need to. Under his suntan his face grew flushed, and he shifted uncomfortably from one foot to the other.

"You *did* know!" Elli gasped.

Reluctantly, Sam nodded. "I knew," he admitted.

"But how? When?"

"My grandfather," Sam replied softly. "He told me one night last summer. I don't know how he knew—maybe from your grandmother. I couldn't believe it, either. I couldn't—"

"You knew all this time that Mr. Ransom was

my father," Elli cut in, shaking from the jolt of betrayal, "and you didn't *tell* me?"

"How could I tell you something like that?" Sam protested, "when I knew a scene like this would happen?"

He put a placating hand on her arm, but Elli writhed from his grasp. "It's my life, and you kept it a secret," she cried, her eyes flashing with anger. "You had no right!"

"I was trying to protect you."

She didn't care about his reasons. Only the bare facts mattered. "You knew and you didn't tell me," she repeated, tears welling up in her eyes.

She wanted to run away, but all at once, she felt limp and defeated. This time when Sam touched her, she didn't have the strength to push him off. "I'm sorry, Elli," he said hoarsely. "I'm truly sorry. God, if I could have spared you this pain . . . What can I do to make it up to you?"

"There's nothing anyone can do," she sobbed, beating a fist against his chest. "Nobody can fix this mess. You can't go back in time and stop my mother from loving Mr. Ransom."

"We can't change the past," Sam agreed, stroking her hair, "but what about the present? What can I do for you now?"

She stepped back from him, wiping her eyes. *Now,* she repeated to herself. *The real problem right now is Ethan and Charlotte,* she realized with fresh anguish. "We have to break them up," she said with renewed conviction. "If we could get Charlotte away from Ethan, I'm sure she'd do something sensible—give the baby up for adoption, or not have it in the first place. We have to break them up," she repeated.

Sam blinked. "We?"

Elli hadn't even noticed she'd said *we* instead of *I*. But she knew she couldn't do it alone. *And he owes me. He owes me.* "You have to help me."

"What can *I* do?"

"It's been no good talking to Ethan, so we have to try to get through to Charlotte," Elli said urgently. "And you— She's always— You have more influence with her than anybody."

"Influence," repeated Sam, frowning.

"You know you do," Elli pressed. "She . . . she looks up to you. Please, Sam. You said you wanted to make it up to me, didn't you? Well, this is how you can. Do something to get Char away from Ethan. Anything. Whatever it takes."

Sam's eyes bored into hers. At that moment there was a loud cracking sound. Behind them, the boat shifted on its supports, teetering precariously. Sam dove under it, cursing as it crashed against his shoulder.

"Are you all right?" Elli frowned with concern, though she stayed where she was.

When the boat was steady again, Sam stepped away from it, gingerly rubbing his shoulder. "I think I pulled something," he grumbled. "But forget about that. Elli, you can't really be serious."

"I am," she declared fiercely.

For a long moment they stared at each other. Dusk was falling, wrapping them in a heavy, ominous silence. "You're mad at me for keeping that secret from you, and now to make it up to you, you want me to break up Ethan and Charlotte," Sam said at last. "You want me to use my . . . influence."

Elli nodded.

"Do you know what you're asking me to do?" Sam's voice shook with emotion. "Do you understand the implications for you and me, Elli?"

Again she nodded stubbornly.

Pain contorted his features. "And is your brother really worth it?"

Tears spilled over, wetting Elli's face like rain. Ethan or Sam. She didn't want to make the choice, but she didn't see any other way out. Again she thought, *He owes me.* "If you really do love me . . . prove it," she whispered.

Sam held her gaze, his eyes also bright with tears. He took a step toward her, but Elli turned her face away, not letting him touch her.

When she looked up again, Sam had disappeared into the dusk. Elli's tears started to flow faster. She leaned her arms against the *Morning*

Mist and sobbed as if her heart would break. Sam's words echoed in her mind, tormenting her. *Do you know what you're asking me to do? Do you understand the implications for you and me, Elli?*

Elli knew all too well. She'd sacrificed him—she'd sacrificed their love. She'd sent Sam straight into Charlotte's arms.

9

Sam pounded his fist against his bedroom wall. *This is crazy*, he thought, pacing the room. *This just can't be happening. Sane, normal people don't do stuff like this to each other.*

But nothing was sane or normal anymore, Sam had to acknowledge. Elli had been right about that much. The circumstances were extraordinary.

In his distraction, he stumbled against the foot of his bed, cursing as he kicked it. "Okay, Elli," he said out loud. "You want me to break them up? I could do it in a minute. You'd be shocked at how easy it would be."

And it *would* be easy. All those passes she'd made at him over the years—Sam knew Charlotte had always wanted him, still wanted him despite Ethan and the engagement. *All I have to do is crook a finger,* he thought, *and*

125

she'll come running. Poor Ethan will be history.

Yes, Charlotte Ransom wanted him. Maybe just because he was the one guy at Silver Beach she hadn't had yet, the last notch on her bedpost. But she wanted him. The problem was, Sam didn't want her, not even a little bit. *Because I love you, Elli Wells. And I thought you loved me. So why are you making me do this?*

Desperately, he thought back on the scene with Elli, searching for some indication that he might be mistaken about what she was after. It was useless. She'd made it all too clear. *Break them up . . . do whatever it takes . . .*

I was trying to protect her, keeping that secret about her parentage, but instead I hurt her, Sam realized. *She thinks I betrayed her.* And she'd left him only one way to reestablish his devotion: save Ethan from Charlotte . . . by stealing Charlotte from Ethan.

Sam sank onto the edge of his bed, burying his face in his hands and rubbing his burning eyelids. The whole situation was so twisted and senseless. He was supposed to prove his love for one girl by turning to another girl. *And then what?* he wondered. *When I've gotten Charlotte away from Ethan, what do I do with her? And what happens to Elli and me? Or have we already broken up? Is that what was happening back on the beach? Were we saying good-bye?*

"I won't do it," Sam declared, jumping to his

feet. "I won't take Charlotte if it means losing you, Elli." But even as he spoke the words he knew they were futile. If he refused to intervene, if he didn't do what Elli had begged him to do, she'd never forgive him. She'd never forgive him for two things: for hiding the truth from her, and for abandoning Ethan to his fate. With a sinking heart, Sam realized his choice was no choice at all. Either way he lost the girl he loved.

Sam made his way across the room and reached for the telephone on the nightstand. Picking up the receiver, he dialed the number at Briarwood.

Charlotte ducked out the side door of Briarwood and glanced across the lawn. The coast was clear: no sign of Ethan, who'd moved back into his family's house when Charlotte's father returned early from his book tour. A smile of anticipation on her face, Charlotte dashed up the driveway just as Sam's Mustang rolled to a stop.

The engine idling, Sam leaned over to push open the passenger-side door for her. "Hop in," he invited.

Charlotte slid in, pressing her short skirt against her slender thighs so it didn't ride up too high. Her heart was fluttering rapidly. She couldn't remember the last time she had felt this excited, this stimulated. Or this intrigued. Why had he called her?

Sam flashed her an easy smile. "Sure this is okay?" he asked. "You weren't planning to go to the costume ball?"

Charlotte and Ethan did have a date to go the Midsummer Madness costume ball together, and he'd be coming by Briarwood any minute now to get her. But she wouldn't be there, and she hadn't phoned or left a note explaining her absence. "No, we didn't have any special plans tonight," she told Sam.

"So." Sam gunned the engine, and the Mustang shot down the gravel lane toward the main road. "I thought maybe we could just go for a drive, stop somewhere for a bite to eat if you're hungry."

"Sounds good to me," said Charlotte.

They drove for a few miles in silence, the radio turned up loud. Finally Charlotte couldn't sit still a moment longer. Bending forward, she turned down the volume, then faced Sam. "Why did you call me?" she asked bluntly.

Sam stared at the road ahead of them in silence. Waiting for his answer, Charlotte studied his profile. A muscle twitched in his jaw.

Abruptly Sam swung the car onto a dirt road that led to a town beach north of the summer colony. They rolled to a stop in the deserted parking lot and he killed the engine and the lights. Charlotte held her breath. "I don't know why I called you," he began, staring straight ahead, his hands still resting on the steering wheel. "No, that's not true," he exclaimed an instant later. "I called you because . . . I just wanted to spend some time with you. Some time alone with you. I've been . . . worried about you."

"Worried about me?" Charlotte raised her eyebrows. "How come?"

"Because of, well, the reason you and Ethan got engaged. And that's another thing." Sam cleared his throat. "I can't stand the thought of you marrying him. It's been driving me crazy."

Charlotte was baffled. "Why should you care what I do? It never bothered you before, me and Ethan."

"It bothers me now," said Sam. "I guess until this happened I . . . I never knew how I really felt about you."

She stared at him in disbelief. Was Sam DeWitt really saying these things to her? After years of holding her at arm's length? "Sam," said Charlotte softly. "Does this mean . . . ?"

"I don't want you to marry Ethan," he said gruffly. "I want—I want—"

"What?" She placed a hand on his knee. "What do you want?"

For the first time, Sam turned and looked at her. In the dark, his expression was hard to read, but his words were plain enough. "You," he said simply.

"Oh, Sam," breathed Charlotte. She felt his

hands on her shoulders and she melted toward him, her whole body flooded with a sudden, throbbing heat. How often had she dreamed of this, of being alone with Sam, of touching him, kissing him? *At last,* Charlotte thought. *At last.*

She wrapped her arms around his lean waist and lifted her face to his. "I've loved you forever," she whispered, brushing his lips with hers, teasing herself by holding back from the kiss she desired more than anything in the world. "But you knew that."

Sam chuckled low in his throat. "You dropped a few hints."

"And you finally picked them up." Charlotte slid her hands up Sam's muscular back under his shirt. "I've waited a long time for this."

"Let's not wait any longer." She felt his lips on her hair, her temple, her cheekbone, the corner of her mouth.

She couldn't hold back another second. She placed her mouth firmly on his, her lips parting to taste him hungrily. The kiss grew deeper and even more delicious. He crushed her body in his arms, his strong fingers probing her shoulders and neck, tangling in her long, loose hair.

"We have to get out of this car," Charlotte murmured at last, her lips traveling down to the pulse in Sam's throat. "No room to maneuver."

"There's a blanket in the back," said Sam.

Charlotte stepped out of the Mustang and

waited for Sam to retrieve the blanket, shivering with pleasure and impatience. Sam straightened, the blanket in his arms, and looked across the car at her. "C'mon," she urged, her eyes glowing.

He didn't move.

"What's the matter?" Charlotte asked.

"I think . . ." Sam placed a hand on the car door, which he hadn't closed all the way. "I think I'd rather take you home."

She smiled, her teeth flashing white in the dark. "You're right. The beach is for locals. I've always wanted to see your bedroom at Eagle Cottage."

They drove back to Silver Beach in silence that was tense with expectation. Charlotte kept one hand on Sam's body, massaging his shoulder, his biceps, his knee, his thigh, her fingers light and caressing, full of passionate promises.

To her surprise, he turned into the driveway of Briarwood. "I don't think this would be the best place," Charlotte told Sam. "I mean, Ethan might—"

Sam climbed out anyway, leaving the engine idling in neutral. Charlotte followed suit, walking around the car to stand at his side. "Sam, what—"

Quickly, he grabbed her shoulders, planting a hasty kiss on her lips. Another rapid movement and he was behind the wheel again. Its tires spitting gravel, the Mustang tore off . . . without Charlotte.

*　　*　　*

Elli threw her book down on the living room sofa. Leaping to her feet, she hunted for the television remote control. After a few minutes of channel-surfing she turned off the set and gave her novel another try. It was no use. Nothing could distract her from the agonizing thought that Sam might be with Charlotte at that very moment.

Maybe they went to the ball, she thought, looking out the window in the direction of the yacht club. *I could walk over there and just take a peek.* She preferred the thought of them being together in a public place. If she could see them with her own eyes doing something harmless like dancing, then she wouldn't have to imagine other scenarios: a moonlit walk on the beach, a drive in Sam's car, a tryst at Eagle Cottage . . .

Elli stepped out onto the porch. Two voices floated through the dark, immediately gripping her attention. She flattened herself against the shadowy wall of the house, listening.

"What do you mean, leave you alone?" Holling Ransom demanded. "You called me back early from my trip, and now you're sending me packing like some rejected suitor?"

"I just need some time to myself," Elli heard her mother say in reply. "Just for tonight. To think things over."

"To think *what* things over?"

132

"I don't know. Maybe I need to think about . . . us."

For a long moment Mr. Ransom didn't respond. Elli held her breath in suspense. At last he said, "That sounds ominous, Grace."

"I didn't mean it to," she said, her tone placating. "But Holling, I can't deny that I've been, well, distressed by how you're handling this thing between Charlotte and Ethan. Or rather, not handling it."

"I don't want to have this conversation again," said Mr. Ransom. "Maybe I *should* go home."

"Yes," said Mrs. Wells, her voice shaky. "Maybe you should."

Elli heard footsteps on the creaking porch stairs. A tall, dark figure started across the lawn toward Briarwood.

Noiselessly Elli let herself back into the house. She climbed the stairs to the second floor, thinking she'd take a long, hot shower to relieve her tension. As she walked down the hall Ethan emerged from his bedroom. "How come you're not at the ball?" she asked him, dreading the answer even though she knew it in advance.

"Char stood me up," said Ethan with an awkward laugh. "Isn't that weird? I looked everywhere for her." He raked a hand through his hair. "Maybe it's one of those moody pregnancy things and she just didn't feel like partying. I don't know why she'd blow me off and hide out, though."

Elli bit her lip so hard she tasted blood. *I know where Charlotte is,* she wanted to shout out, *and I know whom she's with.* A wave of regret washed over her. *I did this. I pushed Sam into Charlotte's arms.*

The idea of Sam with Charlotte was intolerable. What had she been thinking? "Maybe it's not too late," she whispered.

"What?" asked Ethan. "I didn't hear you."

Elli whirled around, not answering him. She leaped down the stairs in a few long strides and raced for the door. Maybe it wasn't too late to take back what she'd said to Sam that afternoon, to beg his forgiveness. Maybe it wasn't too late to save the love that, she realized now, meant more to her than anything else on earth.

Sam turned back the covers on his double bed, wincing at the pain that shot through his left shoulder. *I really wrenched it, catching the boat from falling this afternoon,* he thought, rubbing it gently. *Strained a ligament or something.*

He turned off the light, then stepped over to the window. His bedroom was on the first floor, the windows opening out onto the porch. Sam pushed the sash up as far as it would go to let in the night breeze, then pulled the curtain. After shedding his clothes, he climbed naked between the cool cotton sheets.

His adrenaline was still pumping from the encounter with Charlotte. *Man, is she going to be pissed this time,* Sam thought. He felt bad about the way he'd treated her—leading her on, then ditching her and driving off like that. She'd opened up her heart and he'd responded callously. But he just hadn't been able to go through with it.

Not that I didn't come close. A feeling of shame washed over him as he remembered. For a few seconds there, he'd really gotten into their make-out session. *It was sexy,* Sam admitted to himself, tossing in bed. An intense physical curiosity had swept over him. Charlotte was Elli's half sister, after all. But the point was, he'd stopped—he'd known, ultimately, that he just had to stop.

I'll explain to Elli first thing tomorrow, Sam determined. Maybe she'd be disappointed; maybe she'd be mad. But he'd make her see that he loved her too much to leave her for Charlotte or any other girl, no matter how compelling the reason. They'd just have to come up with another way to help Ethan.

Slowly Sam's body relaxed and his eyelids drooped. He drifted into dreams of Elli. He didn't know how long he'd been asleep when a sound woke him. The curtains had been drawn back from the window, and they fluttered in the wind.

His eyes blurry with sleep, Sam hitched himself up onto one elbow and blinked in the darkness.

Then a shadow shifted and he drew in his breath sharply. Someone else was in the room, standing just inside the window.

"Sam," a voice whispered.

The figure—a girl—moved forward on silent feet. She dropped something on the floor—a robe—and then he could see that she was naked, her body gleaming softly in the darkness.

"Elli," Sam murmured as he sank back on the pillows, unsure if he had indeed woken up or if this was still a dream.

It was no dream. The girl reached the side of his bed, and he smelled the sweet musk of her skin as she lifted the sheet. Then her warm body was pressing against his. "Elli," Sam said again, fully awake now. He focused on her face, expecting gentle blue eyes, a curtain of silky shoulder-length brown hair, a delicate, smiling mouth.

The eyes were blue, but they were slanted and gleaming like a cat's. The lips were fuller, redder than Elli's. And the hair that spilled across his pillow was golden.

The girl in his bed was Charlotte.

Elli raced down the porch steps, hardly noticing that Mr. and Mrs. Wells were sitting in the rockers, talking. As she sprinted up the dark road toward Eagle Cottage, one of her sneakers came untied and she tripped over the lace. She knelt to retie it, panting, and then sprang to her feet again, running faster to make up for lost time.

I'll tell him it was a mistake, Elli thought, light-headed from emotion and exertion. *Temporary insanity or something. I didn't know what I was doing, throwing him at Charlotte like that. I want him to stay with me forever. I'm in love with him. How could I forget even for a second that I'm in love with him?*

When she spotted Sam's car in the driveway, Elli's heart filled with hope. He hadn't gone out after all. Maybe Charlotte's standing up Ethan didn't have anything to do with Sam—maybe Sam hadn't taken any action yet.

She was about to knock on the front door of the cottage when she remembered how late it was. Sam's grandfather was probably asleep. *Maybe Sam's asleep, too,* Elli thought, walking around the side of the house on the porch. Her lips curved in a smile as she anticipated how much fun it would be to wake him up with a kiss.

She reached Sam's bedroom window and paused, her heart pounding at the thought of her own boldness. The curtain was drawn to the side and the window was open wide, even the screen. *All I have to do is climb over the sash and I'll be in his arms. . . .*

The murmur of voices arrested her. "Oh, Sam," someone called out.

Elli's blood froze in her veins. She knew that voice; there was no mistaking it. Charlotte.

Elli drew back from the window, crumpling at the waist in pain, as if she'd been shot. Charlotte was in Sam's room, in Sam's bed.

She stumbled back down the steps to the lawn, running blindly through the trees to the beach. Charlotte and Sam.

When she reached the sand, Elli sank to her knees, sobbing brokenheartedly. Sam had done what she'd asked him to do, and done it thoroughly. He wasn't just distracting Charlotte a little bit. He'd gone all the way.

10

Ethan was waiting on the steps of Briarwood
when Charlotte returned home, on foot, at
dawn. All night long, he had been as taut with
strain as a guitar string; at the sight of her, he
nearly passed out with relief. "Where have you
been?" he exclaimed. "I've been so worried
about you!"

Charlotte approached at a leisurely pace.
"You shouldn't worry so much," she said, stretching her arms over her head. "I was just . . . out."

"Where?" A second question died on his
lips—a question too horrible to ask. *With whom?*

Charlotte gazed at him, her blue eyes cool
and depthless. "Do you really want to know?"

Ethan blinked. Her tone told him that he
didn't want to know, that he should have stayed
home, his back turned to Briarwood. But he *had*
to know. "Yes," he whispered hoarsely.

Charlotte smiled with a look of ultimate satisfaction—a cat who'd just lapped up a bowl of the sweetest, richest cream. "I spent the night at Eagle Cottage," she announced. "With Sam."

Ethan's knees buckled as if he'd been kicked. He leaned back, clutching the banister with one white-knuckled hand. "With *Sam?*"

"That's right." As Ethan watched in confusion and disbelief Charlotte slipped the ring he'd given her from the fourth finger of her left hand. "Here. You can have this back."

"I don't want it back," said Ethan.

"Let me put it another way," said Charlotte blandly, still holding the ring in midair. "The engagement is off."

Numbly, he took the ring. "But Char." Ethan's voice cracked. "I love you."

She shrugged. "Sorry about that."

He lunged forward, gripping her shoulders. "You can't just walk away," he cried. "What about the baby? Our baby?"

Charlotte reached up and brushed off his hands as if she were slapping away a bothersome gnat. "There is no baby."

"What?"

"It was a mistake. I got my period. I'm not pregnant after all." Pushing past him, she climbed the porch steps. "And now, if you don't mind, I'm going to get some sleep. I'd appreciate it if you didn't hang around and make a scene." The door slammed shut behind her, and a bolt slid heavily into place.

Ethan backed away from the cottage, wild eyes fixed on the locked door. *This can't be happening,* he thought desperately. But Charlotte's words left no room for doubt or argument. She wasn't pregnant; they weren't getting married. She'd dumped him . . . for Sam.

Elli was sitting alone in the breakfast room, cupping a mug of lukewarm, untasted tea between her hands, when the screen door squeaked open and Ethan shuffled in. Without a word to Elli, he straddled a chair, dropping his head on his arms. For a long moment she watched his broad shoulders shake with suppressed sobs. "What is it?" she said at last, even though she already knew. "Ethan, what's wrong?"

He lifted a pale, tortured face. "I hate to be the one to tell you this," he croaked, "but it's— it's about Sam. Sam and Char. They . . . got together somehow." He dropped his head again, mumbling into his arm. "She broke up with me, El. Just now. She said—she said—"

Elli waited, a feeling of dreadful certainty blossoming in her stomach like a poisonous flower. It was true, then. She hadn't been mistaken about what she'd heard as she stood outside Sam's window the night before.

"It turns out we're not having a baby, so we

don't need to get married, and Char . . . she spent the night with him. How could she do that to me?"

Elli's calm facade broke. A spasm shook her body. She knocked over her mug, splattering the table with lukewarm tea. Ethan's eyes, now filled with compassion as well as grief, fixed on his sister's face. "I'm sorry," he muttered. "God, I shouldn't have just come right out and said it like that. This is as rotten for you as it is for me. We've both been betrayed."

Elli turned her head to hide behind a curtain of hair. Her brother's heart was broken. How could she tell him that she had known this was going to happen, that she had *made* it happen? How could she tell him she was the betrayer rather than the betrayed?

"I'm sorry, El," Ethan repeated. The chair scraped against the floor. She felt his hand rest on her shoulder briefly. Then she was alone again.

No one else was up yet and the house was still, so she could hear Ethan's steps in the hall, on the stairs, in his bedroom directly above the breakfast room. He was home—home to stay. He wouldn't be going back to Briarwood ever again.

Elli stared at the puddle of spilled tea, her eyes dull and dry. She wanted to cry, to sob and scream, but she couldn't make a sound; she was a statue, frozen, dead.

Ethan had been saved from Charlotte, who

wasn't even pregnant. He wouldn't get married and become a father while still in high school. Elli had her brother back. But at what price?

"It's classic Char. Really unbelievable," Heather Courtland declared in disgust. She slung an arm around Elli's shoulders, giving her a consoling squeeze. "Like it's not enough to pull a total one-eighty and dump Ethan flat after getting him to ask her to *marry* him. She has to go after Sam, too."

"I can't believe she finally got her claws in Sam." Amelia Madden shook her head. "I really thought he had more sense."

"I'm sorry, Elli." Becky Nichols's eyes were warm with sympathy. "If there's anything we can do to cheer you up . . ."

The girls were having lunch on the deck of the yacht club. Elli had hoped to have a day or two of grace, a little time to come to terms with what had happened to her and Sam, and to Sam and Charlotte. She thought Sam would come to her and explain, reassure her somehow.

Instead, he'd gone public. Or at least Charlotte had gone public. By midmorning everyone in Silver Beach had heard about Sam and Elli's breakup and Sam and Charlotte's wild night together. Now the two of them were eating hamburgers and fries in the Little Club, looking very much the hot new couple.

Elli sipped her cranberry juice. "I guess I really don't want to talk about it," she mumbled.

"I don't blame you one bit," said Heather. "Subject closed, okay, everybody?"

Becky and Amelia nodded. Elli finished her juice, then balled up her napkin and rose to her feet. "See you later," she told her friends.

Becky patted her arm. "Keep your chin up."

Elli repeated the advice to herself on her way to rejoin her day campers. *Keep your chin up, keep your chin up.*

Elli had been avoiding Charlotte for many reasons: her anger about the engagement, and then the weirdness of learning she and Charlotte were related. Knowing that Charlotte had spent the night with Sam made it a million times worse—Elli never wanted to lay eyes on her again. But at that very moment, Sam and Charlotte were tossing their garbage out and walking toward the clubhouse exit. Too late, Elli realized that they were on a collision course—there was no place to hide.

She continued walking, her chin up and her face flaming. Charlotte's arm was hooked possessively through Sam's. When she saw Elli, a smile as bright as a sunrise broke across her face. Elli couldn't help staring at them. Silver Beach had probably never seen such a stunning, glamorous couple. *But they can't be a couple. It wasn't supposed to go that far. He's supposed to be mine,* Elli thought, pain searing her heart. She choked back the accusing words that rose in her throat. She knew Sam had only done what she'd asked him, begged him to do, but still. *How could you?* she wanted to cry. *How could you?*

Sam kept his eyes on the floor—he didn't even say hello as he passed. Charlotte's smile widened as the two of them walked through the clubhouse door.

He's not just going through the motions, Elli thought, discreetly dabbing at a tear. *After all, he's still with her, even after he managed to break up the engagement. He must want to be with her.* And why wouldn't he? Wasn't Charlotte the most desirable girl in Silver Beach? *My half sister—like me, but better.*

For a long moment Elli stared at the clubhouse door. Even when she opened it and stepped out into the sunshine, something still seemed to stand in front of her, blocking her path: a wall cutting her off from everything that had gone before this terrible day, from her love for Sam and his for her. A wall, too tall to scale, standing between her and all their wonderful plans for the future, their dreams.

Charlotte laughed as she and Sam left the clubhouse and crossed the lawn.

"What's so funny?" asked Sam.

"Elli's face. Have you ever seen anyone look

145

so *forlorn?* Like somebody shot her dog." She laughed again. "I wish I had a lipstick as red as her face turned just now when she saw us."

"Hmm," Sam mumbled.

Charlotte tightened her arm around his waist. "You're not sorry, are you?" she purred. "About what happened last night."

"No," said Sam, smiling briefly into her eyes. "No, I'm not."

"I didn't think you would be." She pressed a kiss against his cheek. "That's what gave me the nerve to go over to your house. Deep inside, I knew we wanted the same thing."

"Yeah."

In the distance, Charlotte spotted Ethan scurrying toward the tennis courts, his shoulders hunched with misery. All around her, people were staring and whispering. She sighed blissfully. Life just couldn't get any better than this. Everyone was dancing to her tune, suffering because of her—she'd brought the arrogant, overprivileged, self-righteous Wells family to its knees. And, finally, Sam DeWitt had recognized her superior charms. *I beat her,* Charlotte thought, the victory making her feel as high as if she'd just drunk a bottle of champagne. *I beat her at last.*

Sam was quiet. Charlotte jiggled his arm. "You're not thinking about Elli, are you?" she asked. "Feeling sorry for her? Having second thoughts?"

"Uh, no," he said.

"Good." Charlotte stopped walking and turned so that she and Sam were face to face. She wrapped her arms around his neck. "Because I don't want you to think about anyone but me." She knew she only had to say it to make it so; now that Sam had made love to her, he'd never go back to Elli. She stood on tiptoe to kiss him on the mouth, deliciously aware that they were in plain sight of everyone sitting on the yacht club deck. "Is it a deal?"

"Deal," said Sam, kissing her back.

Sam stepped on the gas and the Mustang's engine purred responsively. He was driving to his job in Pentwater at twice the speed limit, but he didn't care. He couldn't get away from Silver Beach—and Charlotte and Elli—fast enough.

Maybe I won't go back, he thought. It was almost the end of summer. He could head to campus, move into the dorm early.

Sam slammed the flat of his hand against the steering wheel, hating himself for his cowardly impulse. "You didn't even have the guts to look at her, you jerk. You didn't even say hi."

When he got to the office, he ducked into his cubicle and picked up the telephone. *I'll call her,* he determined. *I'll explain that it's not really how it looks between Char and me.* He dialed the number. It rang twice and then someone picked up. "Hello?"

It was Elli's voice. Sam's stomach flipped. "Elli, it's me," he said gruffly.

There was a long, horrible moment of silence, then a muffled click and the dial tone. She'd hung up on him.

Just as well. Sam clenched his jaw, replacing the receiver with a sigh of defeat and self-disgust. What had he planned to tell her? Not the truth. Not that Charlotte had climbed into his bed and they'd had sex. All summer, he'd been holding back with Elli, the girl he loved, waiting for just the right moment, and then he'd let Charlotte Ransom seduce him in about five seconds flat.

And like it or not, that had created a bond between them, an obligation. *Life's not like a videotape. I can't rewind and erase last night,* Sam reflected. *You make the bed, you lie in it.* He was tormented about hurting Elli's feelings, but he had Charlotte's feelings to think about now, too. He'd started it. He'd sent Charlotte a message and she'd responded. He remembered the previous night, shame flooding his veins. They'd slept together—he couldn't just discard her.

He knew that Charlotte expected him to come over the minute he returned from Pentwater. *We slept together last night, and we probably will again tonight.* The prospect made

Sam's stomach churn with a sickening combination of desire and despair. It was no use. Maybe part of him wanted Charlotte, but it was the wrong part. Most of him, the best of him, still wanted and loved Elli, and nothing would ever change that. But he couldn't ask Elli to take him back after what had happened with Charlotte. Sam slumped at his desk, his eyes dull and lifeless. He was just going to have to accept the consequences of his actions. There was no way out.

When Elli spotted Mr. Wells sitting on the front porch with a book a few days later, she ducked around the side of the house to the garden in back. Her grandmother was weeding her vegetable patch.

Elli settled onto a bench to watch Mrs. Chapman work. "How come Dad's sticking around?" she asked.

Mrs. Chapman straightened, leaning against her hoe. "He must have a reason."

Elli rolled her eyes. "Obviously."

Just a few days earlier, Elli would have been happy to have her father stick around. *But Dad's not really my dad,* she reminded herself. Mr. Wells wasn't her biological father, and he didn't even know it. He'd always been so loving and supportive. Elli couldn't bear to look at him now, thinking about how badly he'd been duped.

Elli felt something surge painfully inside her and she knew she couldn't suppress her knowledge any longer. The burden of the secret was breaking her in two. "Nana," she began.

"Yes, dear?"

"Dad—I mean, Mr. Wells. Arthur. He's . . ."

Mrs. Chapman tilted her head to one side, frowning with confusion.

"I know about . . . myself," Elli continued. "That he's not really my . . ."

Mrs. Chapman put down the hoe. Removing her gardening gloves, she sat down on the bench next to her granddaughter, placing a thin but strong hand on Elli's arm. "Dear, do you mean to say that—"

"I heard Mom and Mr. Ransom talking," Elli confirmed, "and then I asked her if it was really true and she told me that, yes, Mr. Ransom was really my father and he's always known that, but Dad—Arthur—never knew and—" Elli buried her face in her hands. "It's so sick and confusing. I wish I'd never found out. How am I supposed to live with this? How am I supposed to act?"

Mrs. Chapman rubbed Elli's back, sighing. "Myself, I'd hoped you'd never find out. There seemed no reason to tell you the truth. But sometimes secrets refuse to stay buried."

Elli lifted her tearstained face. "You knew, back when it happened?" Even as she spoke she remembered Sam's confession. *Of course*

Nana knew. That's how Mr. DeWitt found out, how Sam found out.

"I knew that Grace and Holling were falling in love again," said Mrs. Chapman. "Or rather that they had let their love repossess them. And when Grace discovered she was pregnant, and then when you were born . . . She didn't have to tell me. I could see for myself."

Elli stared at her grandmother. She'd always suspected that Mrs. Chapman knew everything there was to know about everyone at Silver Beach. *But I didn't realize my own family harbored so many passionate secrets.* "I'm tired of being kept in the dark, Nana. I want to know everything," Elli declared. "Tell me the story— the *whole* story. Please," she added softly.

"The whole story," Mrs. Chapman mused. "Does any one person know the whole story when it comes to something like this? I can only give you an onlooker's version. But here it is." She drew a long, deep breath. "You know now that as a girl, your mother was in love with Holling Ransom."

"When she was my age," said Elli.

"Even younger," said Mrs. Chapman. "Let's see, when did it start? I believe Grace was fifteen and Holling a year older."

"Like Ethan and Charlotte two summers ago!"

"A bit like that," her grandmother affirmed.

151

"Yes, the two relationships have their similarities. Grace and Holling seemed so young to be so wildly attached to each other, and he was a moody young man. The artistic type, you know, even then. I'm afraid Horace and I weren't terribly supportive of the romance."

"Did you try to keep them apart?" asked Elli.

Mrs. Chapman laughed ruefully. "We tried, but it was like trying to keep the lake from touching the shore. Impossible."

"But then you sent Mom away to school."

Mrs. Chapman nodded. "A year of boarding school, and then a women's college in New England, far away from where Holling was pursuing his studies. And it worked. When she came back to Silver Beach those summers, she was a different girl. Of course, it helped that Holling wasn't around—he spent his vacations hitchhiking around the country with his bohemian writer friends. When Grace began dating Arthur, we were so delighted! Such a nice, good-looking, reliable boy, and a law student—he'd take good care of her. We thought we couldn't ask for anything more."

Suddenly, fragments of a conversation she'd had with her grandmother a few summers earlier popped into Elli's head. "A safe choice," Elli said out loud. "You told me once that Mom had made a safe choice that wasn't so safe after all."

Mrs. Chapman arched her slender eyebrows.

"Did I say that? Well, it's true. Arthur was the safe choice. And I don't want you to get the wrong impression—Grace *did* care for him. But Holling was still in her blood like a drug, and she was in his. Poor Arthur—he really didn't stand a chance. And poor, poor Annette. An uneducated, blue-collar girl. Lovely, but she never came close to satisfying him on any level."

"Why did Mr. Ransom marry her, then, if he didn't love her?" Elli asked.

"He must have thought he loved her," Mrs. Chapman speculated. "And Grace had married someone else. Maybe it was spite, to show Grace he didn't need her, either. But of course he did need her. They needed each other. And the affair started again." Mrs. Chapman's eyes became shadowed. "The risks they took to be together—they were so young, so foolish."

"And careless." Elli's throat constricted. "Mom got pregnant . . . with me."

Mrs. Chapman put a hand to Elli's face, gently stroking her cheek. "You were a love child."

"How could they have been carrying on like that, without Mrs. Ransom and Dad finding out?"

"You know how it is," Mrs. Chapman replied. "Often people don't see what's under their noses because they don't *want* to see. I think both Annette and Arthur had their heads buried pretty deeply in the sand."

"It's so weird—Charlotte and I growing up right next door to each other," Elli whispered. "Half sisters, only we didn't know it."

"Every summer, Grace and Holling would try to stay away from each other, to no avail," Mrs. Chapman continued. "And then came the summer when you and Charlotte were eight years old."

"The summer Charlotte's mother drowned herself," Elli added. "Because she found out about the affair, right?"

"She found out," her grandmother confirmed. "About the affair . . . and about something else."

Elli's eyes widened. "You mean . . . ?"

"I don't know the details, but somehow Annette guessed about your parentage, and of course that was proof that the deception had been going on for years and years. She confronted Holling and he didn't deny it."

"So she waded into the cove." Elli shivered, imagining the depth of the betrayed woman's desperation. "She swam out and just let herself sink."

"It was a shocking event." Mrs. Chapman shook her head. "Of course, the rest of the colony thought it was an accidental drowning, but some of us guessed the truth. It shocked Holling and Grace the most—shocked them into breaking off their relationship. Shocked Grace into trying to save her own marriage before it was too late."

For a few minutes Elli and her grandmother sat on the bench in silence as twilight fell. "The damage had been done, though," Elli said at last. "Mrs. Ransom was dead, and Mom and Dad . . . they didn't stay together. Mom eventually went back to Mr. Ransom."

"Now they're both free—they can openly have what they secretly desired for so many years."

"But they're not happy," said Elli.

"Maybe it would have been different for them if they'd married when they were young," Mrs. Chapman mused. "Sometimes I blame myself for everything that happened later. If Horace and I hadn't stood in their way . . ."

"You were just trying to protect Mom, to be good parents," Elli argued.

"But I should have known better." Mrs. Chapman smoothed a hand over the pair of gardening gloves that rested on her knee. "Because, you see, I had a similar experience as a young girl."

"You?" Elli blinked at her grandmother in surprise. "You were in love with somebody your parents didn't approve of?"

"A handsome local boy." Mrs. Chapman's eyes sparkled mischievously. "His name was Teddy."

"Teddy? Not . . ." Elli's jaw dropped. "Not Ted DeWitt, Sam's grandfather!"

"The very same," Mrs. Chapman said. "Oh, was I taken with him! But he was a working-class youth—his father was the colony handyman. He simply wasn't an acceptable suitor for the pampered youngest daughter of Newland and Anna Pierson."

"So your parents separated you from him the way you separated Mom from Holling," Elli concluded.

"They did indeed. And I went along with it like a sheep. I was an obedient child—it never occurred to me to question Mama and Father's wisdom."

"But you married Grandpa," Elli pointed out, a little hurt at the implied slight to her beloved grandfather. "He was the most wonderful man in the world!"

Mrs. Chapman smiled softly. "I can't argue with that assessment, my dear. He *was* wonderful, and just the husband my parents had hoped to find for me. When Theodore returned to Silver Beach a number of years later, I didn't even blink."

"Even though he'd gotten rich?"

"It was an astonishing transformation," Mrs. Chapman conceded. "No longer just the son of the handyman, Theodore had made millions in the automobile business. He was able to buy the biggest house in the colony, Eagle Cottage. No one could look down on him anymore—he had the money and the power to shape the world to his desires."

Elli studied her grandmother's profile. "But money couldn't buy him everything. He couldn't have you."

"No." Mrs. Chapman sighed. "He wanted me to leave Horace, but I wouldn't. I was a devoted wife, and by that time a mother too. No, I was the one thing he could never own."

Elli thought of her grandmother and Mr. DeWitt's card games, their cups of tea, the bird-watching walks. *Is there anything more? Now that your spouses are both dead, have you fallen in love again?* She didn't ask, though she was burning to know. It was just too private.

"All these stories—everything's so tangled," Elli said instead. "Thwarted romances and clandestine affairs. Broken hearts, suicide." She thought of her own generation's love triangles: Ethan and Charlotte and Sam; her and Sam and Charlotte. "And it never ends, Nana." Her voice quavered. "It's still happening."

Mrs. Chapman placed a hand on top of her granddaughter's. "Destiny," she said, her tone resigned. "Life is a drama in many acts. We don't write or direct it—we just move about the stage, responding to cues we often don't understand. You have to let these things play themselves out, dear."

Elli couldn't help wondering. Was that really the lesson to be learned from her mother's history, from her grandmother's? Was that the lesson of Silver Beach, that she should just stand passively by and watch her true love slip away?

11

Heat lightning crackled in the distance, illuminating wind-tossed trees. Ethan and Elli slouched on the porch steps of the cottage, slurping chocolate milkshakes their grandmother had just whipped up in the blender. "It's going to storm," Elli commented.

Ethan nodded. "Not tonight, though. Maybe tomorrow."

"Every summer seems to end with a big storm," she remarked. "Have you noticed?"

Ethan thought about two summers earlier, when he'd rescued Charlotte from wave-swamped Blueberry Island during a near hurricane. "Yeah. I've noticed."

They sat in silence for a few minutes, spooning the last of the ice cream from their glasses. Then Ethan said, "Do you think it's strange, the way Dad's hanging around? It's been a week."

"I guess," his sister replied. "Kind of."

Ethan gave her a sideways glance. "You say that like you hadn't even noticed."

"I noticed. It's just that . . . I don't know. I haven't talked to him much since he's been here. I'm kind of . . . avoiding him." Elli placed her empty glass on the step beside her. "Ethan, I need to tell you something," she said.

He lifted an eyebrow at her somber tone. "What? Something about Dad?" he guessed. "About Dad and Mom?"

"Sort of. But not about what's going on now. About what was going on a long time ago, before I was born. Before they got married, even."

Ethan waited for his sister to continue. Elli laughed awkwardly. "You'll never believe this," she said. "I mean, talk about truth being stranger than fiction. It's like something out of a soap opera."

"Okay, okay, I'm dying of curiosity," he confessed.

Elli looked over both shoulders, as if to make sure no one else was in earshot. Then she took a deep breath. "Ethan, Dad isn't my— He isn't my father."

Ethan stared. "What are you talking about?"

"He's not my father," she repeated. "I mean, not my biological father. Mr. Ransom is."

Ethan dropped his glass and spoon, and they bounced down the steps to the grass with a clatter. "What in hell are you talking about?" he exclaimed in disbelief.

"It's true."

"B-but how do you . . . when . . ." Ethan stuttered.

In a calm, detached voice, Elli told him the whole story. When she was finished, Ethan realized his jaw was hanging open. He closed his mouth, then opened it again to say, simply, "Wow."

"It's kind of a lot to lay on you," she said apologetically, "but I just thought you should know. I mean, this is your family, too. I'm your sister. Your half sister," she corrected herself.

"You're my *sister*," Ethan stated. He socked her lightly in the arm. "Forget the half part— that's bull. I mean, maybe it's true—how did you say it?—biologically. But that's not what counts."

"It counts for something," Elli said sadly. "It matters. It had to have affected Mr. Ransom's relationship with his wife and with Charlotte. Mrs. Ransom killed herself over it! And maybe Dad never found out, but his marriage with Mom was wrecked all the same."

Ethan had to nod in agreement. "I guess you're right. Wow."

"That ice cream made me cold." Elli retrieved her glass and stood up. "I'm going inside. Want to play cards or something?"

"I think I'll sit out here a while longer." Ethan

161

laughed wryly. "You've given me a lot to think about."

His sister entered the house, the screen door slamming shut behind her. Ethan wrapped his arms around his knees, staring out into the night. Another jagged bolt of heat lightning split the dark sky. In the brief flash of light, a figure was illuminated, crossing the lawn from the beach.

"Hi, Dad," said Ethan as his father approached. "Cool night for a walk, huh?"

"I like the lake when it gets a little frisky," Mr. Wells agreed. "Reminds me of the ocean, without the salty smell."

He sat down next to Ethan on the porch steps. Out of the corner of his eye, Ethan studied his father's profile. *He's not Elli's dad,* he thought. *Now that I think about it, she does look more like Mr. Ransom. Incredible.*

"I've missed Silver Beach," Mr. Wells continued in a musing tone. "Didn't think I would. It's not in my blood the way it is in your mother's." He chuckled. "I married Silver Beach rather than being born to it. But the place grew on me over the years."

Ethan stared at his father, wondering how he could make small talk when so much was going on around them. The question burst from him before he had time to think it through. "Why are you still here, Dad? The thing between me and

162

Charlotte is over. Why don't you go back to Chicago?"

Mr. Wells smiled serenely, not at all surprised by the blunt question. "I found out, after I arrived, that I had other reasons for being in Silver Beach. It wasn't just because I was worried about you."

"Other reasons?" Ethan repeated. "Like what?"

Mr. Wells smoothed his khaki trousers over his knees. "I guess spending time with your mother is the main one."

Ethan couldn't help laughing. "Spending time with *Mom?* Isn't it a little late for that? I mean, you guys are divorced."

"It's late, but maybe not too late," Mr. Wells replied quietly.

Ethan felt as if his heart had momentarily stopped beating. He stared at his father. "Dad, you don't . . . You two aren't thinking of . . ."

"I always backed off from our problems," Mr. Wells reflected. "Retreated into my work, especially those last few years before the divorce. The office seemed like a safer place than home, than dealing with your mother, the changes, what was going wrong between us. I didn't fight for her, son. I didn't fight to hold on to my family, and so I lost you."

"You didn't lose us, Dad. Not me and Elli."

"I'll always be your father, but I *did* lose you

163

in an important way," Mr. Wells insisted. "I lost the idea, the reality, of the four of us together, a family. That family was the foundation of my life, the bedrock. More important than any job could ever be. And I've realized that I can't just replace it someday with a second family—a second wife, more kids. I love your mother. I want her back."

Ethan couldn't believe he was hearing this. He stared at his determined, impassioned father, whose manner was usually so calm and unflappable, so dry and lawyerly. Ethan's chest felt tight with hope. "Do you really think that there's any chance that she'll—that you'll . . ."

"We'll see." Mr. Wells rose to his feet. "Like I said, I'm just learning what's worth fighting for. Doesn't mean I'll win." For a moment he rested a hand on his son's head. Then he too disappeared inside.

Ethan continued to sit on the dark porch, his mind whirling with the revelations of the evening. His father's final words rang in his head like a trumpet, a call to arms. *I'm just learning what's worth fighting for.*

What's worth fighting for. Ethan's eyes focused on the white, gabled cottage across the lawn to the south: Briarwood, Charlotte's house. *She ditched me for Sam and I didn't fight for her,* he realized. *I just lay down and let it happen, let it run right over me and flatten me.*

"Maybe it's not too late for us, either, Cha. Ethan murmured out loud. "Maybe it's time for *me* to take a stand."

Early the next morning, Elli carried a cup of hot tea to the living room and stood looking out the picture window. A low bank of slate-gray clouds scudded across the horizon. White-capped waves dashed against the shore.

"A good day to stay inside and play cards and do puzzles," said a voice behind her.

Elli hadn't noticed her mother, curled up on the couch. "We'll be showing videos at day camp, that's for sure," she replied.

Mrs. Wells patted the sofa cushion. "Sit down, honey."

Elli sat on the sofa, tucking her feet up under her.

After a moment, Mrs. Wells took a sip of her own tea and then cleared her throat. "There's something I think you should know," she began. "Holling and I . . ."

Are getting married, Elli thought, the color draining from her face.

". . . are breaking up."

Elli blinked. This news was even more shocking than an engagement announcement would have been. "You're *breaking up?*"

Her mother nodded. "I guess I should say we broke up, past tense. It's over."

How can it be over after more than twenty years? Elli wondered, dazed by the unexpected news. "I don't know what to say, Mom. I'm sorry, I guess. I mean, if *you're* sorry. Are you?"

Mrs. Wells lifted her shoulders. "It was my decision. The relationship wasn't working, and it was getting clearer all the time that it would never work in the long term."

"But . . ." Elli struggled to understand. Her mother sounded so resigned and matter-of-fact, as if she'd broken up with somebody she'd been dating for a month or two instead of the love of her life, the man with whom she'd had a child out of wedlock, for whom she'd left her husband. "You've ended things before. I mean, there were times when you tried to stay away from each other. But you always got together again. That was your destiny, right? So how can you decide now that it won't work?"

Mrs. Wells's eyes grew distant. "It's so hard to know what matters most. I guess for a long time I had the wrong idea about what would make me happy."

"The wrong idea." Elli couldn't suppress the note of anger in her voice. "You mean you broke up our family by mistake?"

A pained frown creased her mother's forehead. "I wouldn't put it that way. Then again, maybe you're not so far off. I've loved Holling almost all my life, and two summers ago, when

Arthur and I split up, I thought I was going after what my heart had desired most for decades. Finally we could be together openly. It should have been a dream come true."

"Why wasn't it?" Elli pressed.

Mrs. Wells thought for a long moment. "Maybe it couldn't be a dream come true because it was *already* like a dream."

"What do you mean?"

"A secret love affair isn't reality. We never had to deal with our relationship on a day-to-day basis," Mrs. Wells explained. "So, there we were, not romantic kids anymore but a man and a woman, stubborn and set in our ways. The passion was still there, but passion . . ." She sighed deeply. "It's simply not enough."

Suddenly Elli recalled a conversation she'd had with her grandfather a few summers earlier, just a month or so before he died. She'd been trying to figure out what was happening between her parents and he'd shared his own personal theory about the different kinds of love: grand passion versus love built on devotion and companionship, more solid but less exciting ground. *Maybe she had to get a divorce from Dad to appreciate him,* Elli thought, a sad, bitter ache in her heart.

Mrs. Wells continued to muse aloud. "Holling is so unpredictable and, even though he loves me, so . . . solitary. Of course, that's what fascinated and attracted me. But for the rest of my life?" An involuntary shudder ran through her body. "And he was never a true father to Charlotte. He wouldn't have been a good parent to you either, though he did favor you over her. But could I lean on him when times got tough? Could I count on him to be there for me, or would I always come in second to his art?" She gave her daughter a small smile. "All this came to me little by little, Elli, until finally I had to face what it added up to."

"And now you're alone. You don't have anybody." Tears filled Elli's eyes. *Just like me.*

Mrs. Wells reached for a box of tissues and offered them to her daughter. "I'm sorry things haven't gone well between you and Sam, honey."

"The worst part is, it's my own fault," said Elli. "I can't blame anyone else." All at once, she couldn't wait to unburden herself, to receive her mother's healing sympathy. Quickly she confessed that she'd asked Sam to intervene between Charlotte and Ethan in order to break up the engagement. "I knew what would happen, and I pushed him to it. It was all to help Ethan—I thought he mattered most. But I'm miserable without Sam. How could I be so stupid, Mom?"

Mrs. Wells smiled sadly into her daughter's eyes. "No matter how old you are, how much experience you have, it's not easy to know your own heart. I'm proof of that."

Elli blew her nose on a tissue. "Don't you wish you could go back in time, Mom? Make different choices?"

"I don't know about going back in time," replied Mrs. Wells. "But I'll tell you one thing. Sometimes you get a second chance to do things right. You set off on the wrong path, and miraculously it brings you full circle—back to the place you started, or somewhere near it."

"Back to Dad," said Elli with a flash of insight.

A wistful smile flickered across Mrs. Wells's face and her cheeks turned faintly pink. "We're taking things slowly. It's too soon to say, but . . . a reconciliation isn't out of the question."

Impulsively Elli leaned over to hug her mother. "I hope it happens," she whispered, her throat choked with happy tears. "I really, really do." Then she sat back again, biting her lip hard. "It would be so great to be a family again— though I guess we're not really a family, not the way we should be. Mr. Ransom's my real father." She laughed harshly. "I should be sad, then, that you broke up with him. I shouldn't want you to get back together with Dad!"

Mrs. Wells gripped Elli's hands firmly in her own. "I decided I should be totally up front with Arthur so we could start with a clean slate." She took a deep breath. "Last night I told him that you are Holling's daughter."

The color drained from Elli's face. In that moment she realized this was what she'd feared most. She'd lost Sam, and now she was going to lose her father. *He won't love me anymore. How could he?* "W-what did he say?" she stammered.

"He said he suspected the truth long ago, when you were born," Mrs. Wells replied softly. "But it never made a difference. He loves you, Elli. You *are* his daughter in all the ways that really matter, and he's your father and always will be."

Tears welled up in Elli's eyes again. She pressed her face against her mother's shoulder. "Oh, Mom."

Mrs. Wells stroked Elli's hair. "Speaking of straightening things out—you know what you have to do, don't you?"

Elli smiled through her tears. "I have to straighten things out with Sam, the way you're doing with Dad."

"It won't be easy," said Mrs. Wells, "but if you don't try, you'll never know how happy you might have been."

After a hot shower, Ethan towel-dried his hair and combed it smooth. Then he put on a clean polo shirt and his least-rumpled khaki shorts, brushed his teeth, splashed aftershave on his face, and stuck his feet into a pair of loafers. He felt like a soldier preparing for battle. Silently he chanted an inspiring mantra. *Worth fighting for, worth fighting for . . .*

He started across the lawn toward Charlotte's house, his strides long and sure, arms swinging, head up. Halfway there, he saw that someone else was on his way to Briarwood: Sam.

Ethan stopped in his tracks, his face hot with embarrassment. The last person he wanted to bump into was Sam, who also looked distinctly uncomfortable on seeing Ethan. *I'll wait till later,* Ethan thought.

Then he saw Charlotte standing on the porch, watching the scene with undisguised pleasure. She'd never give him another chance if she saw him back down now. A surge of pride heated his blood. *You have to fight for her,* he reminded himself, clenching his fists tightly at his side.

The two boys faced each other on the path to Briarwood. "Clear out of here, DeWitt," Ethan said, his voice hoarse.

"What for?" asked Sam, though not belligerently.

"I need to talk to her. Alone."

For a few seconds Sam stood his ground. Ethan felt the muscles in his arms bunch reflexively. *Maybe I'll have to fight literally,* he thought, anticipating the sensation of his fist smashing into Sam's jaw.

Sam took a step toward Ethan. Then he stopped, shrugged his shoulders. "I'll be back in ten minutes," he said coolly. "And you'd better be gone."

He'd won—this round at least. With a burst of confidence, he strode toward the cottage where Charlotte waited, not speaking or making a move in his direction, a half-smile flickering across her face.

"Charlotte," Ethan began, mounting the porch steps. He hadn't planned out what to say, but the words came easily, as if he'd given this speech before. "This has gone on long enough. Sam just can't care for you the way I do—no one ever will. I love you, Char. I miss you. Please—"

Please. Give me another chance. Take me back. Suddenly Ethan heard himself speaking, as if he were a third person standing off to the side and listening in on the scene. A wave of self-disgust washed over him and he bit the sentence short. He blinked his eyes fast, clearing them of the tears that threatened to spill down his face, marking him as a helpless, lovesick child. He looked at Charlotte, straight on and dry-eyed.

She was still smiling, her full lips curved with gratified delight, as if she could taste each word, as if the words that were so bitter and heartfelt for him were just pieces of candy for her. *She loves this,* Ethan realized. *This is what she wants, to see me squirming, jerking around like*

172

a puppet on a string. Me and Sam both—she's got us both jumping.

Again his father's words came back to Ethan. *I'm just learning what's worth fighting for. The family was the foundation of my life, the bedrock.*

All at once, the memories flooded over him. Ethan thought back over the years and all the things he'd done for Charlotte, and the way she'd treated him in return: the petty cruelties of childhood, when she'd picked on him for not fitting in, dared him to do dangerous stunts to prove to her that he wasn't a weakling; then, when they were older, cheating on him with Sloan Hammond, seducing him away from Laura, and now breaking their engagement to go out with Sam. *Our relationship isn't like bedrock, it's more like quicksand. I've never been able to trust her,* Ethan realized with a jolt. There had always been as much—at least as much—pain as joy, and it would never stop. If he begged her to take him back, as she surely expected him to, he'd be telling her that this was okay, this was the way it should be.

And it's not okay. Ethan stared at Charlotte's beautiful face, her taunting expression.

She stepped into the silence. "I just don't know, Ethan," she said, flipping her lush blond hair over one shoulder. "Maybe Sam's the right person for me now."

Her tone was discouraging, but something in her body language contradicted it. She seemed to soften; he felt her melt ever so slightly in his direction. *Teasing me,* he thought. *Inviting me to beg, to grovel. She wants me to give her the whole performance.*

Slowly Ethan smiled. Charlotte blinked in surprise, her own smile wavering. Then, without responding to her last remark, Ethan turned on his heel and walked back down the porch steps.

He headed toward his house, his pace relaxed and unhurried, though he noticed that Sam had lingered at the edge of the lawn, watching, though he could feel Charlotte's eyes burning into his back. "Ethan!" she called after him, indignant.

He didn't stop. *It's not okay, the way she treats me,* he repeated to himself, the conviction growing with every step he took. *It's not what I want for the rest of my life. I deserve better.* Charlotte Ransom would always be the most exquisite, desirable woman in the world, and the most conniving and selfish. *She'll never change,* thought Ethan. *But I can change. She's not the only one who can walk away.*

He knew without looking over his shoulder that Sam had mounted the porch steps and taken Charlotte in his arms. And though this knowledge still caused him pain, the twinge wasn't as sharp as it had been the day before.

The next day it would be even fainter, duller, until finally, someday, the hurt disappeared altogether.

The prospect buoyed Ethan's spirits with a new feeling of empowerment. Charlotte wouldn't give up on him right away. She'd go on expecting him to fall apart, to come crawling back and give her yet another opportunity to lie to him and string him along. Well, she'd be waiting in vain. For once in his life, Ethan had the upper hand. He knew something she didn't: it was really and truly over between them, this time for good, and this time because *he* wanted it to be.

By midafternoon, the storm was closer—the wind that whipped the trees of the summer colony had a shrill, whistling edge to it. Restlessly Elli paced the porch of her family's house, her eyes fixed on the surging steel-gray water of the lake. *I feel like that inside,* Elli thought. *Like there's a storm in my stomach.*

There was only one way to still the waters of her soul. Her grandmother had talked about destiny, about letting things take their course, but Elli knew her mother had given her better advice. If she stood aside and did nothing, nothing would change. Sam would continue to belong to Charlotte. He'd never know how much Elli missed him, how much she regretted telling him to break up Charlotte and Ethan.

A loud cracking sound jolted her from her reverie. She looked north at Gull Cottage in time to see a large branch break off and fall from one of the Emersons' stately old oaks. *Wow, the wind is really getting rough.* Elli shivered, feeling the damp, angry chill through her thick sweatshirt. *It'll probably knock down more than a few trees tonight.*

Suddenly a different image flashed before her eyes: a beautiful blue sailboat torn loose from its moorings and dashed to pieces against the rocks. The *Mist,* thought Elli. Last time she'd seen the boat, Sam had been easing it into the water to test its seaworthiness. What if he'd left it where it would be vulnerable to the wind and the waves?

She raced up the road, her hair flying out behind her. She reached the cove and instantly spotted the blue sailboat. Someone had gotten there before her and was already struggling to drag the *Morning Mist* to sheltered ground. Sam.

For a moment Elli watched from a distance, not sure whether to continue forward or to retreat before he saw her. Now that she had the opportunity to talk to him, she didn't know what to say. Her heart was brimming with longing, but also with anger and hurt. And how could she open up to him when she didn't have the faintest idea what he was thinking or feeling? She remembered the phone call the other day. She'd hung up before he'd had a chance to tell her what he wanted. Had he been calling to explain?

To apologize? To ask her forgiveness . . . or just to tell her a more formal good-bye?

As Elli hesitated Sam paused in his work and winced, rubbing his left shoulder. *That's right,* Elli recalled. He'd hurt his shoulder the other day, when they were finishing up their work on the boat. The last time they were together—the last time they had talked.

Elli drew a deep breath and walked over. Startled by her unexpected appearance, Sam's face reddened and he dropped his eyes before she could read their expression. The cautious greeting Elli had been about to utter died on her lips. Wordlessly she began helping with the boat.

They worked quickly and efficiently. In just a few minutes, the *Morning Mist* was well away from the waterline, snugly tarped and secured to the ground by ropes and stakes. Elli brushed her hands off on her jeans. *Say something, Sam,* she pleaded silently. *It's now or never.*

But Sam continued to avoid her gaze. How could he refuse even to acknowledge her? Elli had planned to make the first move, but now her pride simply wouldn't allow her. The first fat drops of rain began to fall. With one last, anguished look at Sam and at the beautiful boat that had represented their love for each other, the boat they would never sail together, she hurried back to her house.

12

Sam was dripping wet by the time he reached Briarwood. He could have stood outside in the rain all night, letting it wash him clean. *Where's it going to end, this stupid game we're all playing?* he wondered as he stamped his feet on the welcome mat. He clenched his jaw, thinking about Elli down by the boat. He hadn't been able to bring himself to meet her eyes; he was too ashamed of what he'd been doing with Charlotte. And that standoff with Ethan, as Charlotte looked on—like two medieval knights jousting for a lady's favor. It was all beyond absurd.

Charlotte met him at the door, a flannel robe wrapped around her curvy body and her golden hair tousled and loose. "I started a fire in the fireplace," she said, placing a hand on his arm to draw him into the house, "and I made hot chocolate with schnapps. Let's get warm."

Stifling a sigh of resignation, Sam kicked off his sodden sneakers in the front hall. Charlotte led him into the living room, where the fire crackled and the lights were low. When she started unbuttoning his shirt, he recoiled. "What about your dad?" he asked, looking over his shoulder.

"Don't panic," Charlotte said with a throaty laugh. "I won't jump you—just thought you'd be more comfortable if you got out of these wet clothes. And Dad's getting ready to leave on another book tour. He's oblivious."

Sam stripped down to his boxers, then wrapped a blanket around his waist. Charlotte curled up next to him on the couch. "Isn't this cozy?" she purred.

He nodded, wondering how she'd react if he confessed that he'd rather be out in the rain. "Yeah."

"So, let it storm. We'll stay safe and warm right here."

She ran a hand up his arm to his shoulder. Sam shifted uncomfortably. He tried to tune out thoughts of Elli, but it was impossible. "Maybe I should go over to the clubhouse, see what's happening there," he said. "I took care of the *Mist*, but other people might need help shuttering up their cottages, securing their boats."

"The *Mist*." Charlotte sniffed. "What do you care about that stupid old boat, now that you and Elli have broken up?"

Sam shrugged. "We put a lot of work into it. She was there, too."

Charlotte narrowed her eyes. "Just now? Elli?"

"Yeah." A wistful smile flickered across Sam's face. "I guess she didn't want to see it chopped up into matchsticks, either."

Charlotte drew in her breath sharply. "I can't believe she's still following you around. That's what it is, you know. She's trying to steal you back from me."

"I don't think so," Sam said, looking at his hands. "She didn't say a word the whole time."

"She doesn't have to!" Charlotte's temper flared. "She's just so sure she'll get what she wants, and she usually does. But not this time." She dug her fingers into his arm. "I'm not letting you go."

Sam shook his arm free. "This isn't some kind of contest. I'm not a trophy."

"I didn't mean it that way." Charlotte gave him a soft, placating smile, but there was a hard glint in her eyes. "You can't blame me for hating her, though, Sam. Her and her whole damned family. But especially her. So spoiled, so perfect, everybody's favorite. God, she's been a thorn in my side ever since we were kids. I wish she'd never been *born!*"

The words echoed in Sam's mind. *You can't blame me for hating her, hating her, hating her . . . I wish she'd never been born.* Sam looked at the girl next to him—so beautiful and so full of hatred. *That's what it's all about, these vicious games, these twisted love triangles,* he thought. *Feeding the bottomless pit of Charlotte's need and hatred.* It was bad enough that he'd allowed himself to become one of Charlotte's victims, but that Elli should still be her main target!

Sam wanted to shake Charlotte hard, to make her cry and apologize. Instead, he gripped the arm of the sofa, his knuckles whitening. The exclamation burst from him before he had time to think about its consequences. "She's your sister," he declared.

Charlotte stiffened, her wide eyes fixed on his face. "What?"

"She's your sister."

She drew away from him, her shoulders hunching. "My *sister?*"

"Half sister," Sam amended. "You have the same father."

Charlotte turned pale and her upper body swayed. Sam reached out to steady her, but she slapped his hand away. "I don't believe you."

"I'm sorry, but it's true," he said, instantly regretting his haste, his harshness. "I *am* sorry, Char. I shouldn't have—"

"My half sister," she cackled. "My half sister. Of course, it makes perfect sense. The person I despise most in the world, and the same blood runs in our veins. What a taint. What a curse."

I didn't hurt her after all. It's impossible to hurt her. Abruptly Sam got to his feet. Dropping the blanket on the couch, he reached for his damp trousers and shirt and started to dress. "Where are you going?" asked Charlotte, her voice rising.

"I think I'd better leave," he said, zipping his pants. His heart was heavy with guilt and confusion, but one thing seemed perfectly clear: even if he never got Elli back, he couldn't stay with Charlotte. He didn't come close to loving her and she didn't love him. "This isn't going to work."

"What do you mean? What's not going to work?"

"Us." Sam gazed down at her, his eyes cloudy and apologetic. "This."

"Of course it's going to work." She grabbed his hand and tried to pull him back to the couch.

"No." Gently, Sam pried his fingers free. "I'm sorry, Char."

Her eyes flashed angrily. "You can't just walk away from me."

"Please don't make this harder than it already is," said Sam. "I'm sorry. I wish I felt differently, but . . ."

"You still love her, don't you?"

The accusation caught him off guard, piercing Sam's soul like an arrow. "This has nothing to do with her," he protested, though he knew the truth was written all over his face. "You and I aren't compatible, that's all."

"But we could be," Charlotte insisted, clinging to him. "I want us to be, Sam. I don't want you to go back to her. I won't *let* you go back to her!"

"Don't do this," Sam said gruffly. "I'm leaving, Charlotte."

"No," she said, her voice imperious. "No!"

She leaped to her feet, blocking his passage to the door. Sam took a deep breath, then pushed her aside. He felt her fingernails clawing his back, but he didn't stop. He didn't turn back. Yanking open the door, he fled into the stormy dusk. The rain pelted his face, cold and cleansing. He was free.

Charlotte stood in the hallway, her hands clenched into fists and her whole body shaking with rage. How dare he just walk out! Who did he think he was?

Gradually her rage at Sam's rejection gave way to a new fury. The revelation of Elli's parenthood, of their sisterhood, stared her in the face like a cruel, hideous goblin. *I should have known,* Charlotte thought. *I should have known it had been going on forever. I should have known it was more than an affair that killed Mom. And no wonder Dad never loved me. Elli came first—he already had the perfect daughter.*

As stiff as a robot, she turned and marched up the stairs to the second floor. In her bedroom, she dropped her robe on the floor. Not bothering with a bra, she slipped into a pair of tight, faded jeans and a baggy T-shirt. Then she walked down the hall, her eyes glazed.

She entered her father's room without knocking. He glanced up from the suitcase he was packing, surprise and irritation on his craggy, handsome face. "What do you want?"

"I want you to tell me how you could do it," she said. It was weird to hear her own voice, hear how calm she sounded, as if she really didn't care about any of this. She felt as if she were floating above her own body, watching the scene from a safe distance. "How you could father a child with the woman next door and flaunt it in my mother's face until you'd driven her to suicide."

For an instant Mr. Ransom looked stricken. Then he shrugged. "You know about Elli."

"Didn't you think I'd find out someday? Didn't you think everyone would find out eventually? It's disgusting, Dad," Charlotte declared. "It's sick."

"It happens," he said. "And frankly, I don't see how it concerns you."

"You don't see how it concerns me." Charlotte laughed harshly. "You don't see how it concerns me that you were never faithful to my mother, not even when you were first married. That you let your lover raise your child right next

185

door, that you always favored Elli—always. When did Mom find out about your bastard? It was that summer, wasn't it?"

Mr. Ransom dropped a stack of neatly pressed oxford shirts into his suitcase. "Your mother was hysterical, unbalanced. We were having problems, but nothing a mentally stable woman wouldn't have been able to handle."

"So now it's her fault she was so unhappy." Charlotte shook her head in disbelief. "I can't believe you, Dad. I can't believe you're still trying to feed me that crap."

"Charlotte, if you don't mind, I'm busy. I have a plane to catch."

"Look at me, Dad," Charlotte commanded.

Mr. Ransom raised ice-blue eyes to his daughter's face. She didn't want to cry in front of him, but suddenly the tears were gushing uncontrollably. "What about me?" she whispered. "Haven't you ever worried, even a little bit, about how all this affects me?"

Her father's expression was as cold and unchanging as a glacier. "I'll be gone for three weeks on this book-signing tour. You're capable of getting yourself to college, aren't you? I've placed a down payment in your name at the BMW dealership in Spring Valley. Trade in your car for something new, and don't miss the first day of classes."

He shut his suitcase; the lock clicked.

Draping a garment bag over one arm, he lifted the suitcase and walked past Charlotte, leaving her alone in the bedroom.

He couldn't care less, she thought a minute later as she heard his car engine start up. *He's never cared. I could be standing here bleeding and he'd be oblivious to my pain, just like he was oblivious to Mom's pain.* Oblivious to anyone's pain, she realized, even his own. He seemed absolutely numb to the fact that Grace Wells had left him.

As her father's Mercedes pulled out of the driveway, a big gust of wind rocked the cottage, making the shutters jump and clatter. An instant later, the power went out and Charlotte was in the dark.

She crossed to the window, looking out at the storm. With lights extinguished everywhere, the buildings of the colony seemed to disappear, swallowed by the wind-driven rain. *It's like being the last person on earth,* Charlotte thought, hugging herself. *No one can see me. No one will come over to make sure I'm okay.*

Suddenly Charlotte knew in her bones, in her blood, what her mother had been feeling as she swam out into the lake to die. *I'm alone, too. I've been rejected, betrayed. No one loves me. What reason is there to go on living?*

Charlotte stared at the lake as angry waves dashed against the shore. The water seemed to call out to her, to beckon to her. Turning away from the window, she ran across the room, down the hall, and down the stairs.

Outside, the rain was falling so hard and fast it was almost impossible to see. Charlotte ran barefoot across the sodden lawn, splashing mud at every step. She arrived at the cove panting and bedraggled, her wet hair clinging to her face, her clothes already waterlogged. *I'll be so tired and heavy, I won't have to swim far,* she thought. *It'll be easy.*

Then her wild eyes settled on something. A boat—the *Morning Mist.* Hate surged through her body. All at once, she no longer wanted to destroy herself; she wanted only to destroy this symbol of Elli and Sam's enduring love, a love she would never possess. Sprinting to the boat, she yanked off the ropes that secured it and began shoving it toward the churning water.

Elli paced in front of the living room window. "I can't stand it," she burst out suddenly. "I'm going for a walk, Nana."

In the candlelight, Mrs. Chapman's eyes were wide and startled. "You mustn't," she said. "It's not safe."

But Elli was already at the closet, grabbing a slicker. "Dear, please," Mrs. Chapman called after her. "Don't—"

Elli stepped through the door, pulling it tightly

closed behind her. All around her, the night boomed with noises of the storm: the splash and pound of waves, tree branches groaning and cracking, the whistling of the wind. The tumult exhilarated her, responding to the storm in her soul.

The *Morning Mist,* Elli thought fearfully. Had they secured it well enough to weather a storm like this? Suddenly it mattered more than anything that the *Morning Mist* make it through the storm unscathed. *It's all that's left,* Elli thought as she bent her head to the gale and hurried toward the beach. *All that's left of me and Sam. If I lose the boat too . . .*

The colony appeared deserted; everyone was sheltering inside. But as Elli neared the shore she saw a lone figure, wet golden hair whipping in the wind, struggling to push a boat into the surf. The boat was the *Morning Mist . . .* and the person was Charlotte.

Elli froze in her tracks, her heart in her throat. Instantly she knew what was happening. *Destiny.* Her grandmother's word seemed to echo in the night, carried on the ruthless wind. *Is this Charlotte's destiny?* Elli wondered. *To repeat her mother's tragic end, to die by water?*

The boat was nearly to the water's edge. Something tugged painfully at Elli's heart and she rushed forward, one hand outstretched. *I can't let her do it.* "Charlotte, no!" Elli cried, gripping the gunwale of the boat.

Charlotte whirled to face Elli. "You can't stop me!" she shouted.

"It's not worth it," Elli pressed. "No matter what's happened, it's not worth taking your own life!"

"Why should you care what I do?" Charlotte's eyes flashed sparks. "You hate me, Elli Wells. You've always hated me—you'd be happy to see me dead."

"No." Elli shook her head, tears mingling with the raindrops on her face. "I don't hate you, Char. I don't *want* to hate you," she added, more honestly. "I can't hate you. Don't you see? We— you and I . . ." She knew she had to tell Charlotte; she had to tell her they were sisters. But the words stuck in her throat.

To her surprise, Charlotte laughed harshly. "We're sisters," she spat. "Yes, I know."

For a long minute the two girls stared at each other. Elli felt as if she were looking into a dark, distorted mirror. Now that she knew to look for it, the resemblance seemed unmistakable. *My eyes, my face,* she thought. *My sister.*

Charlotte turned away first. Again she hauled the *Morning Mist* toward the water.

Elli made one last plea. "We're sisters," she cried. "I'll—I'll help you. It could be different."

"You'll never be my sister," Charlotte yelled disdainfully. "You may not hate me, Elli, but I hate you and I will until the day I die."

The boat was afloat. Elli leaped forward to hold Charlotte back, but Charlotte didn't even try to climb in. Giving the sailboat one last shove, Charlotte splashed back to shore and ran off down the beach.

Elli stood at the water's edge, looking from Charlotte's fleeing figure to the boat, which was quickly being carried out into the raging surf. "Our boat," she moaned, stamping her foot at her own helplessness.

Then something—someone—brushed past her. A boy was kicking off his shoes and ripping off his jacket. Sam.

He took one look at Charlotte running off down the beach, at Elli, at the *Morning Mist* spinning out into the current. Without a second's hesitation he dove into the stormy water and began swimming after the boat.

"Sam, no," Elli called. "You'll never make it!" But he was already in deep water, swimming doggedly against the waves.

She winced at the thought of the pain he must be in from his sprained shoulder. He didn't seem to be making any progress. How soon before he tired, before the current dragged him under? Elli glanced frantically over her shoulder, hoping she'd see somebody who might help. But there was no one . . . only Charlotte, watching from a wind-whipped dune.

Was she laughing? Elli couldn't see through

the rain. But hot anger poured like lava through her veins, pushing aside the pity she'd felt just a few moments earlier. Once again Charlotte had managed to put herself in the driver's seat. She was in control, gleefully destroying the things that mattered most to other people. *And I was going to risk my own life to save hers,* thought Elli. *Because of blood.*

Elli looked back out over the cove, at Sam, at the boat. And in a flash she understood that although they couldn't be disowned, blood ties weren't necessarily the strongest. Holling Ransom may have fathered her, but he wasn't her father—Arthur Wells was. *And love is about building things together, not destroying things. Building things, like me and Sam and the boat.*

A feeling of strength and confidence flooded Elli's body. As Sam had just a moment before, she kicked off her shoes and pulled off her soaked sweatshirt. She could see that Sam was flagging, his strokes growing more uneven. She ran to the shore. *I can do it,* Elli told herself as she plunged into the cove. *I can save the boat, and save Sam. I'll save us all.*

13

Charlotte sat in the grass, her arms wrapped around her knees. The storm raged around her. She felt as if she were in a bubbling cauldron, spinning and tumbling in the wind and rain. *Fools,* she thought exultantly. *You'll drown— you'll both drown.*

She watched the two tiny figures swimming against the waves after the storm-tossed sailboat. Elli's words came back to her. *I can't hate you. Don't you see? We're sisters. It could be different.*

"Sisters," Charlotte whispered, her throat suddenly tight with tears. Loneliness swept over her, and the memory of loneliness. All those years after her mother's death, with her father ignoring her. The bitter isolation. *A sister might have made a difference,* she thought with a start. *At least I wouldn't have been alone. If only I'd known. . . .*

But she hadn't known. Charlotte swallowed the tears, clenched her jaw. She hadn't known, and now it was too late to feel close to the girl she'd envied all her life. Elli Wells, the daughter Charlotte's father had always favored, living, breathing proof of the affair that had killed Charlotte's mother. *If I have to look at her for the rest of my life, and be reminded of that over and over, I'll go crazy.*

She bent her head, resting her chin on her tucked-up knees, making herself small against the storm. And she watched the two swimmers, praying that they wouldn't reach the boat, wouldn't make it back to shore. It didn't matter to Charlotte that Elli was her half sister. She still wanted her dead.

A wave rose in front of her as high as a wall. As she plunged down into the trough on the other side, Elli glimpsed the *Morning Mist. I'm almost there!* she thought with renewed energy. *I'm going to make it!*

But what about Sam? She paused to tread water, her eyes searching. Then she spotted him just a few yards ahead of her. He was still swimming despite his injured shoulder; it looked as if he too would reach the boat safely.

But as she swam closer an especially large wave crashed over Sam, submerging him completely. Holding her breath, Elli waited for Sam to resurface on the other side.

He didn't. She immediately saw the reason why: a massive piece of driftwood, spinning in the vortex created by the wave. *He got knocked out,* she thought with alarm, choking on a mouthful of water. *Oh my God, where is he?* Then she saw his body rolling limply on the crest of another wave, being carried away from the sailboat.

"I'm coming!" Elli shouted into the wind, forgetting her concern about the boat. Only one thing was important now—saving Sam.

In a few swift, strong strokes, she reached Sam's side. His eyelids flickered; he was partially conscious, but in no shape to swim. *A few more seconds and he would've gone under,* Elli realized as she hooked her shoulder under his and began towing him back toward shore.

She didn't realize how tired she was until she was bearing Sam's weight as well as her own. Her waterlogged clothes dragged on her limbs, and it was all she could do to keep her head above water. She kicked and paddled with all her might, but gradually she could feel her efforts growing feebler. And shore still seemed so far away. *I'm not going to make it,* Elli thought, panicking. *Someone see us, please. Help us.*

Blind with fatigue, she continued to fight her way through the surf. Just as she was ready to give up, to let her body sink beneath the waves, her foot scraped bottom. Now the current worked with her, propelling her and Sam toward the beach.

As she stumbled into the shallows, still cradling Sam's body, Elli felt his arms and legs jerk. Sam was conscious now, and she helped him to the sand. On his hands and knees, he coughed up the water he'd swallowed. Then he rolled over on his back, panting and pale. "Elli," he whispered hoarsely. "What happened?"

She knelt beside him, tears of gratitude spilling down her face. "You went after the boat, and I went after you. You got knocked out. But you're going to be okay," she said, grasping his hand.

His eyes were naked with longing. "I just couldn't let the boat go. I thought it was all I had left to remember you by."

"No," Elli whispered. "You still have me."

"Oh, Elli." Sam reached for her, and she went to him, burying her face against his neck. "I love you so much. You've always been the only one. Do you believe that?"

She nodded, the tears flowing faster. "I love you, too."

Waves dashed against the shore, spraying them with cold water. All around them, the storm continued to scream. But Elli and Sam were huddled in a warm cocoon of love, holding tight to what they'd almost lost forever.

*　　*　　*

Charlotte thought she was going to be ill. It was like a scene from some melodramatic B movie: Elli hauling Sam's battered body to shore, leaning over him. Then the embrace. Even from a distance, even in the rainy dusk, there was no mistaking the passionate abandon. *They're back together,* Charlotte thought bitterly, rising from her seat in the lee of the windswept dune. Sam had blown her off, and now he belonged to Elli again.

The wind buffeted her on the outside, while jealousy and resentment rocked her inwardly. "He never wanted you," she snarled out loud, "it was just some game he was playing with Elli. No one wants you—you might as well have thrown yourself in the lake."

No one wants me, Charlotte repeated to herself. Suddenly she realized with a spark of life that she was wrong. There was one person in Silver Beach who'd loved her unconditionally since the beginning of time, who'd go to his grave loving her.

Her feet carried her instinctively to the Chapman cottage. She pounded on the door, and Ethan himself answered. "Charlotte!" he exclaimed. "What are you doing out on a night like this?"

"I need to talk to you," she answered, hugging herself and shivering. "It just couldn't wait."

His eyes were guarded. *Of course he's a little*

wary, thought Charlotte. *I've hurt him. But as soon as he finds out why I'm here . . .* She had to stifle a smile as she imagined their reconciliation: Ethan's blissful gratitude, the adoring words and kisses he'd shower her with.

"Well, uh, okay." He opened the door wider. "Come on in and get warm."

He led her to the living room, which was lit only by a couple of candles; the power was still out. Rummaging in a closet, he offered Charlotte a fuzzy lap robe. "Here," he said. "Wrap this around you before you catch pneumonia."

"You wrap it around me," she urged.

Ethan kept his distance, still holding out the blanket. Finally she took it and they sat down on opposite ends of the sofa. Ethan waited, his hands calmly folded on his lap.

"I had to come right over," Charlotte began, "when I realized . . . I realized I'd made a mistake." She let her voice dip with emotion. She dropped her eyes, the picture of repentance. "I lost my head. I was just so flattered that Sam was interested in me. But I've been missing you like crazy, Ethan." She slid closer to him, placing a hand on his arm. "I told Sam just now that it's over for him and me. I could never care for him a fraction as much as I care for you."

At Charlotte's touch, Ethan stiffened. Carefully he reached down and removed her hand from his arm. "I'm sorry it didn't work out for you and Sam," he said quietly.

"*I'm* not sorry. Don't you see what this means? We can be together again, Ethan. The way we were before."

She waited for him to break down, his shoulders crumpling with relief, his eyes brimming with happy tears. Instead, he shook his head. "I don't think so."

"Why not?" She edged even closer, pressing her body against his. She caressed his arm, her eyes glowing with love. "Don't you remember how we talked about the future? We belong to each other, Ethan. I hurt your feelings, but I'll make it up to you. And I promise, I'll never—"

"Don't," he cut in. He pushed her away and jumped to his feet. "Don't make promises you can't keep, Char."

"Ethan, give me a chance," she pleaded.

"I've given you chances. Lots of them."

"But I swear, this time I—"

Ethan laughed sadly. "Oh, Charlotte. We both know better, don't we?"

Tears sprang to her eyes. "I don't understand," she cried. "Why are you being so stubborn? Don't you love me? Do you want me to beg? Is that it?"

A shadow darkened his eyes from green to gray. "No, I don't want you to beg. I'm not just teasing you, Char. I'm not toying with you. I'm trying to tell you good-bye."

"Good-bye?" she whispered, staring.

Ethan walked over to her. Standing in front of her, he bent down and planted a feather-light kiss on her forehead. "Good-bye, Charlotte."

Crossing the room, he stood in front of the window with his back to her. For a long moment Charlotte was paralyzed with astonishment. Then she flung off the blanket. "Ethan!" she cried imperiously.

He didn't turn around.

"You can't mean this," Charlotte hissed. "You'll regret this for the rest of your life, Ethan Wells."

She saw his shoulders tense, but still he didn't turn.

Springing from the couch, Charlotte bolted toward the door and stumbled out into the night. The storm hadn't abated. As she ran across the grass to Briarwood, the rain lashed her skin like a whip, and the wind deafened her with its howls. She pressed her hands to her ears, desperate to shut out the terrible noise, but as she reached the porch of her own cottage, she realized that the wailing was in part coming from her own throat. She was sobbing as if someone had taken a hammer and broken her heart into a thousand pieces.

She'd always taken such care to make sure she

stayed detached, in control. She'd absorbed the love and worship of others like a thirsty sponge, doling out her own favors sparingly, keeping her feelings carefully locked inside. "My heart can't be broken," Charlotte choked. "Especially not by Ethan Wells."

Inside, she fell onto her bed, pressing her face into the pillows. Her body shook with sobs. Finally, after what seemed like an eternity, the tumultuous emotions drained away, leaving her limp and still.

She sat up on the edge of the bed, wiping her eyes on her sleeve. The room was dark—the whole house was dark, and empty, and cold. *It's always been like a tomb, even when Dad's around,* Charlotte thought. *It stopped being a home when Mom died.*

But then a memory came to her, a memory of laughter and warmth. It was a sunny afternoon earlier that summer, and she and Ethan were playing hooky from the tennis clinic. They were lying in her bed, tangled up in the cool cotton sheets after making love. Ethan was braiding her long hair and telling her rotten jokes. They were so bad and unfunny that she couldn't help laughing hilariously. Ethan had touched her face with his finger. "You're so beautiful when you smile like that, Char," he'd said. "When you smile with your eyes."

Ethan's the only guy who ever really cared

for me, thought Charlotte. How could she not have recognized this sooner? Why hadn't she appreciated him? *He wasn't just in it for the sex—he loved me. And he knew me, inside and out. He knew I could be a cold, selfish witch and he didn't care. He loved me despite my flaws.*

She saw that day vividly now, she heard their laughter. She'd been happy then. She'd felt safe. "You're beautiful, too," she'd whispered to Ethan. "When you smile like that, with every inch of your body."

Charlotte buried her face in her hands. *It can't be over*, she mourned silently. *It just can't be.* Her stomach twisted with pain as she remembered how firmly Ethan had told her good-bye. As if his love had died and she'd lost her power to move him. *But maybe it was just because he could sense I wasn't being completely sincere*, Charlotte thought, hope rising in her heart. *Now that I've realized how much I've always loved him without even being aware of it . . .*

She turned to the window, looking across the lawn at Ethan's own bedroom window in the neighboring cottage. The curtain was drawn.

On her own windowsill stood the stump of a candle in an old brass candlestick. Charlotte fumbled in the dark for a book of matches. She struck one, and it flared up with a sizzle. She touched the burning match to the wick, then sat back to watch the flame blossom.

It was their private signal. How many times had she lit a candle in her window, only to see Ethan dart across the dark lawn a minute later? Or he would signal first, pulling his shade and then letting it snap up again. *He'll come,* Charlotte thought, the peace of certainty stealing into her soul. *He'll give me one more chance.*

14

Elli and Sam sat at the dining room table bundled in thick terry-cloth bathrobes, woolly slippers on their feet and mugs of steaming jasmine tea in their hands. Mrs. Chapman lifted a kettle of water she'd boiled over the fire. "More?" she offered.

Elli held out her mug. "Thanks, Nana. My teeth have finally stopped chattering."

"You're a lifesaver," Sam told her appreciatively, holding out his own mug.

"I'll heat up some soup next," Mrs. Chapman promised. "And toast some cheese sandwiches."

Elli's grandmother bustled back over to the fireplace. Elli met Sam's eye across the table. She felt him nudge her foot with his. "Hi," she whispered.

"Hi," he whispered back. "Is this okay? Or are

you starting to be sorry you dragged me out of the drink? I still have a lot of explaining to do."

"I have a lot to explain, too," said Elli. She smiled, happy just to be with him again. "But we don't have to hash it all out now."

Sam touched her foot again. "We can take our time," he agreed, "because from now on, Elli Wells, it's going to be impossible to get rid of me."

Ethan drifted in, a distracted frown on his face. "Man, I wish the power would come back on," he grumbled. "It's so depressing sitting around in the dark."

Elli shot a worried glance at Sam, then looked back at her brother. She'd expected Ethan to be hostile toward Sam, or at least surprised by his presence, but he'd barely reacted. It was as if somehow he knew the whole story, of which she herself had only gleaned a few fragments so far.

"Might as well grin and bear it," she said. "The wind is still pretty fierce—the power-company trucks won't start making the rounds until morning."

Ethan walked to the bay window, then gasped sharply.

"What?" she asked. "Ethan, is something the matter?"

When he didn't answer, she crossed the room to stand at his side. Outside, the night was wild and black. There was only one faint spot of light visible: a candle, shining in a bedroom window at Briarwood. *Charlotte's window,* realized Elli. *Their old signal.*

She placed a hand on her brother's shoulder, silently communicating her moral support. Ethan's body went tense. She could feel that it was taking all his will and self-control not to obey the summons.

They sat down again at the table, Ethan purposely sitting with his back to the bay window. "How about a game of cards?" he suggested, his voice cracking from the strain.

Elli found a deck in the sideboard and began shuffling. "We don't really have enough people for hearts. Poker? Gin?"

They decided on poker and she dealt the first hand. After winning the first two hands, Sam joked, "This is my chance to get rich quick—we should be playing for money."

"I'll get Nana's jar of pennies," said Elli, rising. "Be right—" As she passed in front of the bay window, she froze, her hand flying to her mouth. "Oh my God!" she cried.

Ethan leaped up, knocking over his chair. He looked to where Elli was pointing.

Just a short while earlier, there had been only a single point of candlelight emanating from Briarwood. Now the whole second floor of the house glowed with an eerie, flickering light. "Her curtains must have caught fire," Elli exclaimed in horror. "The house is burning down!"

In seconds, Elli and Sam had traded their robes and slippers for boots and raincoats and were chasing after Ethan. The three ran across the lawn, then stopped a short distance from Briarwood to stare in dismay at the spectacle of flames and smoke.

"Was there anyone else home, do you know?" Sam shouted to Ethan.

Ethan shook his head. "Her dad left on one of his trips. She's alone in there!"

Elli clutched Sam's arm, sick with fear. "She'll burn to death," she cried, the flames mirrored in her wide eyes. "What are we going to do?"

"If she's not out by now, she's not getting out," muttered Sam. "Smoke inhalation. It's just spreading too damned fast because of the wind."

It was true, Elli realized. The rain had stopped, but the fierce wind fed the hungry flames. She thought of all the old wooden houses. "The whole colony could burn," she whispered.

At that moment her brother tore away from her side. He ran toward Briarwood, plunging into the smoke. "Ethan, stop!" Elli shouted. "What are you doing?"

"I'm going in after her!" he yelled.

In a few long strides, Sam caught up to Ethan and gripped the other boy's shoulder. "It's too late!"

Ethan wrenched himself free. "I can't leave her in there. I've got to try."

Elli too tried to restrain her brother, but it was no use. Ethan broke away from both of them and disappeared into the conflagration.

Elli turned from the sight, burying her face against Sam's chest. He wrapped his arms around her. "He's crazy. They'll both be killed," she sobbed.

Sam stroked her hair. "It's okay, El—it could be okay. Remember when he went after her in the storm, when she was stranded on Blueberry Island? We didn't think they'd make it then, but they did."

Blueberry Island—Elli had almost forgotten. "Yes," she whispered. "It's just like that." Ethan heroically, foolishly going to Charlotte's rescue even though she'd cheated on him and betrayed him. An incident that had reunited them and sealed their devotion. *Of course, it's happening again,* thought Elli, staring dully at the crackling flames. Now that Sam had come back to her, of course Ethan would return to Charlotte. But could he save her this time? Or would Briarwood become a fiery funeral pyre?

*   *   *

The first floor of Briarwood swirled with black smoke. Grabbing a dish towel, Ethan quickly doused it in the kitchen sink and pressed it against his mouth and nose to keep himself from choking. Then he scrambled blindly up the stairs to the second floor.

He stopped on the top step, buffeted by a wave of almost unbearable heat. Flames were everywhere, dancing and roaring. *It started in her room, so it'll be worst there,* Ethan thought, momentarily panicked. *Maybe Sam and Elli were right. Maybe this is suicide.*

But he couldn't turn back now. He thought of the girl he'd given himself to, body and soul. His first, deepest love. He couldn't turn his back on Charlotte.

Steeling all his nerve and courage, Ethan plunged forward. Flames licked out from the walls, singeing his skin. Coughing, he fought his way down the hall to Charlotte's door. The heat was almost unbearable, but he pressed forward. His eyes smarted, and tears streamed down his face. *I can't see,* he thought desperately. *Where is she?* Had the flames already consumed her?

Then he tripped against something—a soft, limp form. It was Charlotte, collapsed on the floor. Bending, Ethan scooped her unconscious body into his arms and stumbled from the room.

As he reached the bottom of the stairs he felt

Charlotte convulse and start coughing. "Ethan," she choked, clinging to his neck.

"I'm here," he told her, brushing her smoky, singed hair with a kiss. "You're safe."

They emerged from the house, both of them coughing and dizzy from the fumes. Ethan sucked in deep breaths of clear air. All at once, he heard a deafening boom behind them, an explosion like that of dynamite. The roof of Briarwood buckled as if a giant had stepped on it, and he shuddered, thinking that just a minute before, he and Charlotte had been inside.

The sound of sirens was growing louder. A fire truck screeched into the driveway, followed closely by an ambulance. In the meantime, Ethan could see that his family and neighbors had been busy. Wielding garden hoses, Elli, Sam, Mr. and Mrs. Wells, and others were wetting down the nearby houses and white pines most in danger of catching sparks from the Briarwood fire.

Still holding her tightly, Ethan set Charlotte on her feet. She leaned against him, trembling and coughing. As the paramedics buckled her onto a gurney for transport to the hospital, she began to cry, the tears streaking her soot-stained face. "Please come with me, Ethan."

The plea triggered a vague memory, one of Ethan's oldest. He'd only been three years old, and Charlotte four. *She hit me over the head with a hammer because I was playing with a toy she wanted,* he recalled. *Mom and Dad had to take me to the hospital for stitches and I cried and cried until they put Charlotte in the car next to me.* And that was the pattern over the years: no matter how she injured him, the bond between them only seemed to strengthen.

She was looking at him urgently, and he knew it would be too cruel not to go with her. He knew that she needed him. *I'll go with you, but it's not for keeps, Char,* Ethan thought. *Because I don't need you, not anymore.*

He brushed the hair back from her forehead. "I'll make sure you're okay," he promised. "Don't be afraid."

Hours later, as the fire trucks were driving off, a taxi braked at the top of the Chapman driveway. Ethan climbed out, paid the driver, and then walked slowly to the house. In his bedroom, he fumbled in his desk drawer for a small jewelry box, slipping the ring that Charlotte had once worn on the fourth finger of her left hand into his own cool, dry palm. Then he walked back downstairs and out to the lawn.

He saw his sister watching as he crossed the dunes to the beach, but he didn't stop to speak to her. He needed to be alone for a few minutes, alone with what he was about to do.

The sand was dark and damp under his

shoes, the lake still ruffled and uneasy. Ethan stood at the water's edge, gazing out into the infinity of gray and blue. *I can bury something here, and it will be gone forever,* he thought.

Once before, he'd prepared to fling the ring into deep water, but he'd checked himself—he hadn't been able to let Charlotte go. Now he fingered the ring, hesitating. *This isn't the end of your life,* he told himself. *Just the end of one part it. Do it, man.*

In a strong, swift movement, he pulled back his arm and sent the ring sailing through the air. It glinted faintly in the first light of dawn, then slipped beneath the waves.

Ethan stood by the lake for a long minute. When he turned, he discovered Elli standing quietly a few yards away. "I should have done that a long time ago," he said.

"The ring?" she guessed.

Ethan nodded. "I held on to it long after it was worth anything."

For a moment they just looked at each other, their silence laden with understanding. Then Elli asked, "Is Charlotte going to be all right?"

"She thinks she can't live without me, but she'll manage. She's a survivor." Ethan smiled crookedly. "We all are."

Elli touched her brother's arm, then left him alone with his thoughts. Sam was standing on the lawn where she'd left him to join her brother, silhouetted by the dawn sky.

She returned to his side, and he slipped an arm around her waist. Together they gazed at the smoldering cinders: all that was left of Briarwood. "Burned to the ground," said Sam somberly. "But we didn't lose any of the other cottages, thank God."

Elli shivered as she thought about how close the flames had come to igniting her grandmother's house. "It's over." She remembered Ethan's words just now. "We've *all* survived."

"But Silver Beach will never be the same."

Elli knew it was true. "It's over," she repeated, and this time she meant the words in a different way. It was over: the deathly web of love and hate that had bound her family to the Ransoms for generations. Over between her mother and Mr. Ransom, over between Charlotte and Ethan. *And I'll never really get to know them, my father, my half sister.* "They won't come back," Elli predicted out loud. "Holling and Charlotte."

"No, I don't think they will," Sam agreed.

Just then the morning sun crested the treetops. Sam hugged Elli close to him. She took one last look at the still-smoking embers, saying a silent good-bye to Charlotte. To the mistakes of the past. To summer . . . to youth. Then she smiled up at Sam, her eyes bright with love and hope. Together, they turned to face the future.